TERRA NOVA

SETTLING THE
RED PLANET

THELMA RITCHIE

TATE PUBLISHING, LLC

Published in the United States of America

By TATE PUBLISHING, LLC

Scripture taken from the HOLY BIBLE, NEW INTERNATIONAL VER-
SION® Copyright © 1973, 1978, 1984 by International Bible Society.
Used by permission of Zondervan Publishing House. All rights reserved.

This novel is a work of fiction. Names, descriptions, entities, and incidents
included in the story are products of the author's imagination. Any resem-
blance to actual persons, events, and entities is entirely coincidental.

Book Design by TATE PUBLISHING, LLC.

Printed in the United States of America by

TATE PUBLISHING, LLC

127 East Trade Center Terrace

Mustang, OK 73064

(888) 361-9473

Publisher's Cataloging in Publication

Ritchie, Thelma

Terra Nova - Settling the Red Planet/ Thelma Ritchie

Originally published in Mustang,OK:TATE PUBLISHING:2004

1. Fiction-Futuristic/F 2. Age 10 and up

ISBN 1-9331482-5-X $16.95

Copyright 2004

First Printing: December 2004

DEDICATION

To my Lord and Savior, Jesus Christ.

ACKNOWLEDGMENTS

Publishing a book is an amazing process, and one that an author could not complete alone. As such, there are many who contributed to the development of *Terra Nova,* and to them, I would like to express my deepest appreciation.

The beginning ideas for a novel about settling Mars began to collect in my mind while working at a Challenger Learning Center as a mission assistant for simulated space missions with students. Continuing education classes at the University of Washington added to my knowledge about Mars and inspired me to do something with that knowledge. I especially learned a great deal about the Red Planet from Professor James Tillman, a Mars Viking Project investigator, as we collaborated on a module for teachers at NASA's *Live From Earth and Mars* internet site. Further ideas about actually settling Mars were gained from Dr. Robert Zubrin's outstanding book, *The Case for Mars.* I am especially grateful to Dr. Zubrin for generously allowing me to borrow ideas from his book in order to realistically portray a Martian settlement in my story. His book is highly recommended for those readers who want to investigate non-fiction plans for Mars exploration. To all of the abovementioned people and entities, I owe a debt of gratitude for teaching me about Mars and inspiring me to write a story about the planet.

After completing the writing of *Terra Nova,* I enlisted several readers to help me clean up and polish the story. I am most grateful to those who freely gave their time to make the tale a better one. My son-in-law, Adam Richardson, gave me valuable criticism, helping to shape the characterization. He also suggested Terra Nova as the name for my story's settlement. Diana Low, my awesome teaching partner, proofread the book, finding many spelling and grammatical errors for me. Astronomer Extraordinaire, Ed Mannery, read to give me advice on scientific content. In addition, my wonderful husband, Walt

Ritchie, asked tough questions that required some rewriting. The efforts of these four added much to *Terra Nova,* and I am very thankful for their help.

I would also like to thank Dr. Julie Lutz, Director of the NASA Educator's Resource Center at the University of Washington, for writing the Foreword for *Terra Nova.* Dr. Lutz is not only a research scientist, but an outstanding educator, and I am honored that she would take the time to help with this project.

Finally, I am especially indebted to Tate Publishing for believing in *Terra Nova* and giving it the chance to be published. Finding a publisher to even read a manuscript is a rare event for a new author, and I am grateful for being given this opportunity.

TABLE OF CONTENTS

FOREWORD

Thelma Ritchie was passionate about science long before I met her in the early 1990s. She struck me immediately as a person who personifies the phrase "lifelong learner," particularly on science, mathematics and technology topics. Her enthusiasm is communicated well to her students. She empowers them with her belief that every child is capable of learning and of taking pride in the work that they do.

Thelma Ritchie's classroom is full of science projects and displays, many of them done by her students. Producing good science results involves a rich mixture of individual and group endeavors, so she is having the students model science process as it occurs in today's world.

I'm glad to see Thelma Ritchie join the ranks of writers who produce "good science in science fiction" stories, particularly for a youthful audience. Her novel illustrates several things about science and exploration. First, both science and exploration take place in the real world with real human beings who have their own quirks, beliefs and individual backgrounds. The image of a scientist as a totally rational human being isn't accurate at all! I hope that Terra Nova's readers take away the message from the book that science is accomplished by humans who have their own limitations and agendas. And they sometimes even make mistakes, but that doesn't mean the end of their career or their productivity. You don't have to be a robot to be a good (or great) scientist!

Another theme that rings very true in Terra Nova is the notion of science as an international endeavor. As most scientists can attest, modern technology (Internet, digital cameras, etc.) has made possible collaborations between scientists all over the world. I hope that young people reading Terra Nova find this to be an exciting prospect. The internationalization of science means that developing good social and collaborative skills is increasingly important for being successful in a science (or any other) career.

Thelma Ritchie has carefully researched background information on the Martian environment and the issues involved in colonization of the planet and has incorporated them into Terra Nova. Human visits to Mars are not going to occur soon, but scientists and engineers are now able to envision the technology needed to sustain humans on the Red Planet.

Terra Nova incorporates the latest and best ideas about how human colonization might proceed. Why is this important? Why not just dream up a Martian colony that violates physical laws and all that is known about Mars? I think it is important to learn about the world as we read, particularly when we are young and developing our ideas about nature and how things work. Misconceptions about the nature of the world abound and good science fiction books, differentiating them from fantasy books which are clearly not meant to be taken as realistic, are extremely valuable reading material.

Julie Lutz
Research Professor of Astronomy
Director, NASA Space Science Network Northwest
University of Washington

PREFACE

Terra Nova is a work of fiction, but the story presents the hardships and excitement of traveling to and living on another planet realistically. My goal in writing the novel was to create a credible story of inspiration for young readers, with convincing main characters to respect and emulate. In addition, I have attempted to combine the ideas of Christianity with a narrative of adventure that is scientifically accurate and timely. Hopefully, the novel will generate enthusiasm about interplanetary travel, pushing the limits of the imagination.

It is my belief that science and God are not opposed to each other, but that God is in control of creation, and He has given us all of the science that we understand. God's creation is incredibly complex. Mere human intellect will never completely figure it out, but God encourages our spirit of adventure and continually blesses mankind with discoveries about His creation.

Mars is the next frontier, beckoning us to take that bold step of discovery that will lead us beyond our terrestrial world. Even as I thrilled to watch Neil Armstrong put that first human foot on the Moon, I know that others will delight to see a person walk on Mars. It could and should happen in my lifetime. Valid plans for the settling of Mars exist. They are ideas that will work, if mankind is willing to put forth the effort to see them realized. Establishing a base on the Red Planet will truly be the beginning of a "New Earth." Wouldn't you like to be one of the first Martian pioneers? *Terra Nova* presents a brief glimpse of a possible future on Mars.

Read and dream.

LIST OF CHARACTERS

On The Seeker en route to Mars

The Temples: A Christian family who all rely on God; American.

Preston: 46-year-old father; engineer.

Damaris: 44-year-old mother; doctor.

Larraine: 17-year-old daughter.

Andrew: 11-year-old son.

Other Crew on The Seeker

Scott Jamison: 33-year-old pilot; African American.

Tony Davis: 35-year-old navigator; Canadian.

The Crew at Terra Nova on Mars

Rod Sherman: 50-year-old engineer and base commander; American.

Sally Evanoff: 35-year-old biologist and second in command; American.

Rory Galveston: 25-year-old genius and geologist; American; agnostic.

Sammy Yoon: 32-year-old geologist; Korean.

Dmitri Nazarov: 42-year-old mechanical engineer; Russian;

spends time at Red City and alternates duties on the Orbiter with Chang Lee.

Pavel Stanislof: 48-year-old robotic engineer; Russian.

Hiro and Sachiko Tatsuda: 30-year-old twin brother and sister; Japanese. Hiro is a horticulturist and Sachiko is a dietician.

Dieffenbachia Bateman: 33-year-old pilot and engineer; American; spends time at Red City and alternates with Brian Delaney on the Orbiter; oversees life support at Terra Nova.

Sandy Maloney: 34-year-old botanist; American; strong Christian.

Brian Delaney: 43-year-old pilot; British; alternates with Dieffenbachia Bateman on the Orbiter.

Chang Lee: 40-year-old mechanical engineer; Chinese; alternates with Dmitri Nazarov on the Orbiter and assists Pavel Stanislof with robots and rovers.

Remote Crew searching for water in the northern ice cap–the outpost has been nicknamed Red City.

Jenny Colfax: 30-year-old civil engineer; American.

Pierre LaSalle: 36-year-old civil engineer; French.

Max Machiavelli: 40-year-old mechanical engineer; Italian.

Aaron Abrahamson: 37-year-old mechanical engineer; Israeli.

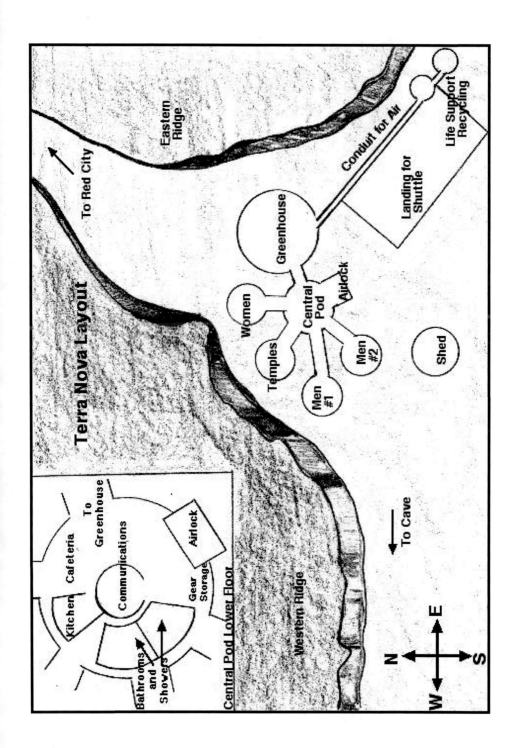

CHAPTER 1

THE STORM

Thwack! Something smacked The Seeker hard. The ship suddenly leaped and the lighting flickered eerily. *What's going on?* Seventeen-year-old Larraine Temple closed the calculus lesson on her handheld computer and met the startled green eyes of her brother, Andrew, who had been working on his history lesson.

"LARRAINE! ANDREW! GET IN THE AIRLOCK NOW!"

The tremor in her mother's voice jolted Larraine. She was convinced that this was no ordinary drill. Her heart thumped like a pounding bass drum as she and Andrew raced for the "tin can" at the center of the spacecraft. *It can't be a solar flare,* she reasoned. *They don't bump into you with force, and we always get warnings ahead of time about them. What could be happening that would cause Mom's voice to sound like that?* As she frantically sped toward the airlock, she noticed a sound like sleet punishing the shell of the spacecraft. *But sleet doesn't exist in the space between Earth and Mars!* screamed her mind.

Andrew was close behind her, but even before they could secure themselves inside the airlock and fasten the door, The Seeker began to shudder. Its tethered rotation was interrupted, as an unseen force slammed the craft. The sleet became hailstones in her mind, while the sound intensified. Larraine was terrified, when an uncontrolled buffeting jostled her from one end of the airlock to the other. Her shoulder hit the wall, and she helplessly fell. Struggling to overcome the invisible force, she grabbed her brother and crawled for the safety wall. She and Andrew fought to tie themselves down, both so intent upon their task that neither was able to ask the other about what was happening. A lot of something was hitting the spacecraft, but what could it be?

Both children finally managed to fasten themselves to the walls of the airlock. They were no longer bouncing into things, but the incessant shower on the spacecraft continued. Larraine looked at Andrew and saw that he had tears in his eyes. She knew she had to be strong for him, because she was the oldest. "Andrew, it will be okay," she assured him. "We knew there would be problems, and we practiced what to do about them. The crew can handle this. They won't let us down." Andrew gulped, as he tried to stop his tears.

Larraine closed her eyes and began to recite part of the *23rd Psalm:*

"*. . . Even though I walk through the valley of the shadow of death, I will fear no evil, for you are with me . . .*"

"But Rainy, we aren't in a valley," Andrew interrupted. "We're in space, millions of kilometers from Earth, and I'm really, really scared."

"God is still with us," Larraine replied. "We have to trust Him." The frightened teenager silently prayed, *You're there, aren't you, God?*

With a last hard *thump,* the buffeting stopped and silence prevailed. The Seeker's course once again smoothed out. Larraine breathed a sigh of relief and smiled. "See?" She tried to sound upbeat, even though her mind continued to wonder what had happened. *Are we still on our course for Mars? Where are Mom and Dad? Is the spacecraft okay?* she asked herself.

Larraine and Andrew both knew that they were not to leave the airlock for any reason until someone came to get them.

16

But how can I stay in here much longer? Larraine protested silently. *I can't see anything, and I can't stand not knowing what's happening. I wish we'd never been picked for this mission. I miss my friends, and at the rate I'm going, I might never see Earth again. I'm too young to die in a spacecraft zooming for Mars.*

Larraine at 17 was a willowy 1.72 meters tall. People told her she was pretty, but when she looked in the mirror, she was not satisfied. She wished her hair was red instead of blonde and curly rather than straight. She desired a longer style instead of the regulation short hair cut for space. She longed to be small, not taller than most of the boys her age. She did agree that her dimpled smile seemed to light her face and her eyes shone a pleasing emerald green, but her nose seemed a little too small and pointy for her satisfaction.

Larraine still remembered the day, twelve months ago, when her mom and dad sat the family down for a serious conversation. She and Andrew were surprised to learn that they had been selected as the first family to go to Mars. They knew their parents, who were both NASA astronauts, had applied for the chance with the Universal Nations Space Exploration Federation (UNSEF), but the odds of being selected were so remote that Larraine had not considered it a possibility. Now she had to recognize its reality.

MARS!
The Red Planet.
The Next Frontier.
Millions of kilometers from Earth.
No water.
No graduation with her friends.
No prom.
What about the church youth group?
Do I really have to go?

There was no question about going. The whole family would either go or not go. This was a very special trip to Mars that UNSEF had been hyping for years. *The first family.* Larraine and Andrew would be the first children ever to travel to and live on Mars. This mission was supposed to prove to the world that people could safely live and work on Mars.

There had already been several manned missions to Mars—one every two years since 2025 (not counting the disaster of 2031). There was even a small settlement established and 16 people living there. People were beginning to think that traveling to Mars was safe and routine, but as a NASA kid, Larraine knew that wasn't true. NASA personnel even joked that the acronym UNSEF was just a couple of letters short of unsafe. There was nothing routine about space travel, even with careful planning and experience. They could easily be the next tragedy.

"Rainy," her brother's small voice interrupted her thoughts. "Why don't they come for us? It's normal again, isn't it?"

"I don't know," Larraine answered. "We have to be patient. They'll come as soon as they can."

"But what if they can't come? What if they're hurt? Can't we go find them?"

"Not yet." Larraine knew exactly how Andrew was feeling. She wanted to check on her parents too. She also knew her parents would expect her to keep Andrew calm in the safest area of the spacecraft. Unfortunately, that was the "tin can" where they could neither see nor hear anything. They both hated spending time in the airlock, and after the fear-inspiring event they had just experienced, remaining inside was almost unendurable. *But necessary,* Larraine reminded herself.

"What's the first thing you want to do when we get to Mars?" Attempting to keep Andrew calm, Larraine tried to make him think about other things.

"I want to climb Olympus Mons."

"Nobody has climbed Olympus Mons." Larraine shook her head. "It's too high, and spacesuits are so cumbersome. You have to pack your air on your back, and you can't carry enough.

Besides, Terra Nova isn't anywhere near Olympus Mons. It's practically at the Martian North Pole."

"I know," sighed Andrew, "but I still want to climb it. Wouldn't it be great to be the first person to climb the tallest volcano in the solar system?"

"We're already first. The first family to go to Mars. The first kids to go to Mars. The first crew to travel in The Seeker. The Seeker is the first spacecraft to leave Earth that can carry six people. How many "firsts" do you need?" Larraine was exasperated.

Andrew smiled, his face resembling Larraine's, minus the dimples. He loved to get his sister going. If the truth was known, that's the only reason he said he wanted to climb Olympus Mons. He knew the idea would set her off. The first thing he really wanted to do was see the robots. Andrew loved machines, and he knew the settlement had a variety of robots to assist the people with their explorations and investigations there. "Well, what's the first thing you want to do when we get to Mars, Larraine?"

Larraine closed her eyes and thought. "I want to see our living quarters and experience total privacy for at least an hour," she responded dreamily. At home, she enjoyed the solitude of her own room, but since The Seeker had left Earth, all 6 crew members had done practically everything together. There was a common room for sleeping, a crowded eating area that was also used for reading, relaxing, studying, and playing games, and one small exercise room. The control room was basically a computerized enclosure where two people barely had space to work. There was seldom a time when anyone was ever alone. Even the bathroom presented a serious privacy challenge.

Suddenly, Larraine and Andrew heard the seal of the airlock door release. The door was pulled open by Scott Jamison, the crew's captain, who looked harried and more scary than usual. The kids were used to Scott by now and knew that his serious demeanor meant nothing. He was really a gentle soul. "Are you kids okay?" Scott's normal swarthy complexion seemed even darker than usual, and his kinky black curls were matted down with sweat. His ebony black eyes looked troubled, as his 2-meter tall, muscular body pushed itself through the small airlock opening. Larraine always thought he should have been a linebacker instead of a spaceship pilot. *How did anyone so huge ever get selected to be an astronaut?*

"We're fine. How about everyone else?" Larraine tried not to sound worried.

Scott appeared grim. "We're all okay, but we aren't sure about The Seeker. That was a pretty ferocious micro-meteoroid swarm. The computer tells us that penetration of the hull occurred. Your dad and I are going to have to go outside to try to repair it, so you kids will need to vacate the airlock now."

"Gladly," said Larraine. "Where should we go? Where is everyone else, and how can we help?"

Scott was frantically opening compartments and collecting gear. "I can't think of anything you could do right now. I can only think about repairing the hull. Your mom is fixing up your dad. Tony's contacting Mission Control and making sure we're still on course. You two should probably just stay out of the way in the activity area." Scott tried to come off calm, but his actions betrayed him as he anxiously continued pulling things out of storage.

"What do you mean, fixing up my dad?" Andrew demanded an answer.

"Look, Andrew, your dad is fine. He just bumped his head hard during the storm, and he needed a few stitches."

As if to prove Scott right, Preston Temple appeared in the airlock with a seriously bandaged head, but otherwise okay. "Dad, are you all right?" The bandages startled Andrew, and he looked like he was finally about to lose it.

"It would take more than a few space pebbles to do me in, Buddy." It was easy to see where both children had gotten their blond hair and green eyes. Preston was the exact opposite of

Scott in appearance. Pale, lean, and lanky, he patted Andrew on the head. "I'm relieved to see that you pulled your sister through in one piece. Pretty shaky ride there for awhile, right?"

"It sure was!" Andrew's eyes were bright and brimming with tears. "It was a lot worse than any simulation we did back on Earth. Can't we go back home, Dad? I don't want to do this anymore. I'm only eleven years old. I'm bored, and I want to see my friends and play with them. I want to run outside, and not only that, I don't want to be pulverized by meteors."

"Meteoroids," corrected his dad.

"Whatever." Andrew looked at Larraine and rolled his eyes.

"You kids know we can't go home. Earth isn't where it was when we left, and there isn't enough fuel to catch it now. We have to depend on orbital mechanics to get us to Mars. Our route has been calculated carefully, and our only possible destination is the Red Guy. I just hope the storm hasn't knocked us too far off course."

"Pres," interrupted Scott impatiently, his dark eyes intense. "I could use a hand here. We need to get this thing repaired."

"Right," replied Preston as he opened the closet for his EVA gear. "Larraine, take your brother to the lounge and keep him entertained while we work on fixing things."

"But Dad," complained Larraine, "we want to help."

"Just do it." Preston Temple turned his back on Larraine and Andrew, closed the airlock, and started changing. Scott nearly had his space suit on, and time was hurtling faster than The Seeker. Who knew how long the damaged hull would hold before it developed a major crack, sending all of their air out into the void?

CHAPTER 2

THE CAVE

Millions of kilometers away, on the planet Mars, a lone man tried to ignore the annoying voice penetrating his thoughts.

"Galveston, come in, please."

Rory closed his cinnamon brown eyes, sighed, and peered into the darkness. His full lips formed a determined frown, accentuating the small dimple in his left cheek.

"Rory, where are you?" yammered the distant voice through his head set. "I'm not kidding. You need to report in right now!" Rod Sherman's voice sounded more than a little irritated.

Rory Galveston continued his investigation at the entrance to the cave and ignored Rod's incessant nagging. He was on a mission, and not likely to be derailed by the ridiculous rules in effect at Terra Nova. Yes, he had memorized them and agreed to abide by them in order to get to Mars, but he had no intention of letting them interfere with scientific discovery. Rory was searching for evidence of life on this planet, and he thought he was on the right track.

Rory and Sammy Yoon had found the area that looked like a washout two weeks before. Following the ridge that formed a picturesque backdrop for Terra Nova, they had walked less than a kilometer to the southwest, and had been surprised to find a break in the towering wall that looked so solid from the settlement. Had a former catastrophic flood burst through a narrow part of the ridge, pushing sediment in its wake as massive boulders collapsed from the walls?

The two geologists had made the discovery before Sammy's sickness had incapacitated him. Sammy was now bedridden and unable to help him explore, and Rory had been chomping at the bit ever since the sol that they had stumbled upon this "former river." So Rory made up his mind that he wouldn't wait any longer. He rose before the sol began, while it was still dark, donned his Mars suit, packed his tools, and grabbed one of the rovers to help him carry things. He left with the rover, even though he knew that exploring on his own was not allowed. He was just not willing to wait any longer.

Besides, having the rover along was almost like having another person. In fact, it was better than having another person along. It helped carry things, moved by its own power, and never interrupted his thinking with silly conversation. If he felt the need to converse, Rory had no problem discussing things with the rover. He even gave it a nickname—N3, for Rover Number 3.

N3 looked a lot like the first rovers sent to Mars back at the turn of the century. The rover had six wheels with a suspension system making it capable of running over everything from pebbles to small boulders. Its front surface was covered with solar cells that gave it unlimited power during sunlit hours, but it also contained a lithium battery, so it could operate for limited amounts of time in darkness. Its back half was basically a wagon for carrying gear, while a 1.5 meter high mast supported a camera that could transmit pictures back to base or even to Earth. The camera lenses gave the impression of intelligent eyes, so it was easy to think of N3 as a living thing. One improvement over the original rover was speed. N3 could travel almost a kilometer in half an hour, a scorching rate compared to its predecessors.

Rory directed N3 along to the washout. With the rover along, it was slow going, but the machine made a great beast of burden. It was an easy distance from Terra Nova, fairly level with mostly small rocks and gravel strewn along the sand. Well, not really sand. The ground was covered with billions of tiny red dust particles called "fines," which were finer than talcum powder. The explorers had learned the hard way that the fines had the ability to get into everything, even things that were supposedly airtight.

Although he enjoyed exploring alone, Rory genuinely liked Sammy, and he missed him on this sol. The short and wiry Korean was a knowledgeable geologist, usually cheerful, and a good friend, despite the difference in their ages. At 35, Sammy was 10 years Rory's senior. *I wish he was here to help me right now. I need to have another geological opinion. Not to mention two more experienced hands.*

Rory was surprised that no one had seen the washout before. *I guess no one ever walked out this way,* he thought. From Terra Nova, the orange, craggy ridge did look like it was all one piece, but Rory and Sammy had found that the ridge was broken, as if a river had cut through it at one time. They also found many smooth rocks and pebbles, a sign of possible water erosion. In order to find evidence of life, Rory wanted to investigate areas that were thought to previously have contained liquid water. Scientists assumed those areas would be the most likely to have fostered bacterial life.

Rory and N3 had meandered along the "stream" picking up rocks to take back to the lab for analysis. Following the stream behind the ridge, Rory had been surprised and thrilled to find a cave on the back side of the ridge wall.

The geologist had left the rover outside the cave, lit his electronic lantern, and eagerly approached the cave to look around. It was a fairly large cave—the entry was tall enough for Rory (who was a decimeter short of two meters) to stand erect. Its width spanned about 3 meters. Moving inside, he found that the walls of the cave were relatively smooth, and from where Rory stood, it appeared that the cave extended back into the ridge. It was impossible to see an end to it from where he was, and the geologist decided he would need to investigate that after taking a few samples. It was easy to see that the cave was more extensive in size than the hab back in Terra Nova that housed as many as 6 men at a time. The cave gave every appearance of being quite roomy, and was the first sizable cave that any of them had found so far on this planet.

Rory was thrilled to find striations of color on the walls of the cave. It looked like there were layers of different types of rocks. Orange-toned layers were interspersed with stripes of charcoal and a cream-colored rock. The scientist had just grabbed tools from N3 and reentered the cave when Rod Sherman's agitated voice broke the solitude again.

"Rory Galveston, answer me now!"

"I read you loud and clear, Commander," sighed Rory. "I'm perfectly safe. I have a rover with me, and I'm less than a kilometer from the base. The weather is clear this sol—not even a hint of a dust storm forming, and I need to explore the find Sammy and I made two weeks ago. It shows lots more promise than anything else we've found during the past year. I've even discovered a large cave that offers all sorts of possibilities for Terra Nova."

"I appreciate that, Galveston. But I am in charge, and it isn't worth losing a man over. You need to show some patience. No one has yet died on this planet, and I don't intend for it to happen on my watch. Dr. Temple is just a couple of months away. Hopefully, she can figure out what Sammy's problem is, treat it with the latest meds from Earth, and the two of you can get back to it. Until then, you have the opportunity to assist with the drilling, out at Red City. I've offered that to you before."

"This can't wait two months, Commander, and I'm not going out to Red City. UNSEF sent me to look for life, not drill holes. Cut me some slack here!"

"Get back here now, Rory. I can't spare anyone to go out with you right now. If I have to leave base to come and get you, you don't want to know the trouble it will cause you," Sherman warned.

"Give me thirty minutes to at least dig out a few specimens to bring back to base with me. I'm already here," pleaded Rory.

"Thirty minutes, and not a second longer. It should take you 45 minutes — tops — to get back to the base after that. If you aren't here by then, I'm coming to get you. I've started my stopwatch."

"Thanks, Commander." Rory turned back to the cave. *All right Rory, get to work. No time to be curious about how far the cave cuts into the ridge right now. Carve out some specimens and get out.*

Rory carefully examined the cave wall. He wanted to cut out a section that included all three striations of color to see if there were three unique minerals making up the wall. He found just the section he wanted, and carefully marked it for cutting. His thirty minutes evaporated as he finally chipped out a shallow section about 3 X 3 centimeters. Rory picked up his tools and light and carefully carried his specimen out to the rover.

"Well, N3, we have ourselves a real find here," bragged Rory. "You just wait and see if we don't. Let's get back to base before Sherman sends out the posse. It's going to take every minute we have to be back when he expects us. Although, I don't know what he thinks he can do to me. It's not as if he can send me home, and he needs every person he has here."

N3, as usual, said nothing.

27

CHAPTER 3

THE INFIRMARY

Less than an hour later, Rory made sure N3 was shut down and carefully replaced with the other robots and rovers in the shed south of the habitats. With his geological specimen in the pocket of his spacesuit, he made his way to the habs, hurrying through the airlock separating the living and working pods from the harsh outdoor, Martian environment. Immediately after making his way through the airlock, he was able to remove the cumbersome spacesuit, and comfortably move around in his regulation Mars jumpsuit.

The electric blue fabric of the jumpsuit was carefully selected to stand out against the drab, dirty white background of the pod walls, adding color and hopefully cheer to an otherwise bleak scene. Every kilogram had to be carefully considered in transport to Mars, so there were no paintings or other amenities to spruce up the décor. The people manning Terra Nova insisted that they were so busy and excited about their explorations, they didn't even notice their surroundings, but psychologists back on Earth worried about their morale. They knew that human beings had an appreciation and need for beautiful things. They were concerned that the lack of color would cause boredom and depression. Because of that concern, the Terra Novan attire boasted an array of bright, bold colors. *If anything, these colors will make us crazy,* thought Rory as he made his way to Sammy's bed.

Rory couldn't wait to tell Sammy about the cave and show him the sample piece. *If anything will make him feel better, it will be this,* he thought happily as he directly approached the infirmary. Rory knew he would need to check in with Rod Sherman, but as far as he was concerned that could wait until after he cheered Sammy up.

The infirmary was an afterthought, having one bed behind some makeshift curtaining. While everyone knew illness and even death was a possibility on Mars, Terra Nova hadn't really prepared for it. Terra Nova's mission was to "Establish, Explore, Discover" and woe to anyone who should be rude enough to hinder that mission by becoming sick. It's true that basic medicines had been sent along, and Sandy Maloney was a registered nurse, but Sandy's main reason for being there was her botanical skill. With a master's degree in botany, she was in charge of the greenhouse, making sure that plants grew prolifically, so Terra Nova's citizens would have food to eat.

Drawing back the curtain, Rory caught his breath. He hated to see his friend growing thinner each sol. Sammy labored to turn his head so he could see who was entering. Each movement he made seemed to require great effort on his part. His breathing was raspy and his voice weak. His black hair looked disheveled from spending so much time against a pillow and his usually alert brown eyes were dull. Seeing Rory, he seemed to take on new life. "Where have you been, Galveston? Rod's been pitching a fit since you disappeared. He's been bugging me, figuring I knew where you were."

"Well, did you?" asked Rory.

"Did I what?" Rory noticed a small spark of mischief behind Sammy's tired brown eyes.

"Did you know where I was?"

"Of course," asserted Sammy. "You were most definitely back at the washout we found."

"How do you know that?"

"Because that's where I would be." Sammy tried to sit up, but was inflicted with spasms of coughing.

"Hey, take it easy," cautioned Rory. He smiled at Sammy and whispered, "You are so right!"

"Well, tell me," demanded Sammy.

"Tell you what?"

"Tell me what you found. I can read you like an old newspaper."

Rory shook his head, amazed that he was so easily seen through. "You're right. I found exciting stuff. I did go back to the washout, and I followed it for a ways. I took its passage through the cliffs, and back behind them there was a cave."

"A cave?" Sammy's excitement caused another bout of coughing. As he caught his breath, he questioned, "Did . . . you . . . go . . . inside?"

"What do you think?" teased Rory.

"I *know* you went into it. Now tell me. What did you find?"

"I'll do better than tell you what I found. I'll show you what I found."

Rory's brown eyes shone with delight as he pulled the specimen from his pocket. The indentation at the left of his chin danced as his face beamed. The tiny piece of rock struck them both with awe as it seemed to shout promise.

Sammy was speechless. "We've never found anything like this before, Sam," Rory informed him. "I plan to start analyzing it to see what we've got here. This could provide some strong evidence for life on this planet."

Sammy's eyes left the specimen and focused to a spot behind Rory's left shoulder. Rory turned around to face Rod Sherman's angry countenance. Rod's normally pleasant blue eyes seemed almost black with anger.

"Where have you been? You should have checked in with me the minute you got back, Galveston."

"Sorry, Commander. I was heading your way, but I wanted to cheer Sam up first."

Rod shook his shiny, bald head as his shoulders sagged with the weight of responsibility. He was in his fifties and by far the oldest person on the base. Rod was overworked, and had no patience for laxity from underlings. "Sorry just doesn't cut it, Rory. You need to follow protocol more seriously, or you won't be here much longer," Sherman steamed. "We don't need renegades up here who think of no one but themselves. You aren't the Lone Ranger. Everything we do is based on teamwork, and this should not come as a surprise to you. I know it was part of your training."

Rory's shoulders slumped and he sighed, "I know it, Commander. Sammy and I made a great find before he got sick, and I've been waiting for him to get well so we could go back. I finally gave up and went back by myself, and I found something pretty exciting." He offered the specimen to Rod.

"What is it?" asked Rod.

"I don't know yet, but we've never seen anything like it here before," answered Rory. "I'm going to start testing and analyzing it right away."

"Well, that should keep you busy and safe for awhile," grumped Rod. "I'm warning you, though. If you pull a stunt like this again, you'll be shipped back to Earth on the earliest possible trip. The Seeker is due within two months. After the ship arrives, it will take about 6 weeks before Mars and Earth are aligned for the journey back to Earth. At that time, we'll be sending 6 people back to Earth, and you just might be one of them."

"But my work here is so important," Rory pointed out.

"And whose isn't?" Rod frowned. "Every person on this base is essential to its success. That's why we can't be taking chances, breaking rules, and exploring on our own. You are not to leave Terra Nova by yourself for any reason. Is there anything about that you do not understand?"

Rory shook his head. "Then who can go with me when I need to go out again? Everyone has a job to do, and no one has time to go with me."

"I don't know," sighed Rod. "Maybe one of the Temple kids can go when they get here."

"No way!" exclaimed Rory. "I'm a geologist—not a baby-sitter."

"It could be a great educational experience for them," mused Rod, and his blue eyes glinted with their normal hue. "I'm liking this idea more and more. Let me know what you find out when you analyze that thing." With that, Rod straightened up and walked off, leaving Rory shaking his head in bewilderment, and Sammy chuckling between his coughs.

CHAPTER 4

BACK ON TRACK

On The Seeker, Larraine and Andrew were not happy. It seemed their mother barely noticed them, as she helped Tony with communication and control. The two of them were forced to hang out in the activity area by themselves. *Does she even care that we're not hurt?* Larraine's mood had gone from dismal to abysmal in the two hours since the clash with the meteoroid storm. She and Andrew had tried to resume their studies, but it was nearly impossible. They were both afraid and wanted assurance from their parents.

Larraine remembered the jealousy shown by her two best friends when they learned that the Temples were going to Mars. "You are so lucky!" gushed Marta, and Lucy nearly jumped up and down when they heard the news.

"But I'll miss the Prom. My only chance to go to the Prom in my whole life," complained Larraine. "I won't get to graduate from high school with you either, and when you go off to college, I'll still be on Mars. I really don't want to go."

"I would gladly give those things up to be at Terra Nova with Rory Galveston," declared Lucy. "He's drop dead gorgeous. And smart. He graduated with his doctorate by the time he was 18 and became an astronaut right away—picked to go to Mars when he was just 23 years old. Unheard of! Just think, you could go exploring for rocks with him on an extra-terrestrial world with a pink atmosphere. How romantic!"

"Come on, Lucy. He's way too old for me. Do you honestly think he would have any interest in taking me on a rock finding expedition? Or that I would have any interest in going on one?"

"Well, I sure would," affirmed Lucy. "Tall, dark, and handsome. Like I said, gorgeous. Not only that, when we go off to college, you get to have your own private tutors and study anything you want. You'll get to spend all that time traveling to Mars earning university credit. By the time you get back home again, you'll have your degree. The first interplanetary university degree! You are so lucky."

I wonder how Lucy would feel if she was here right now? questioned Larraine. *We don't know how far off course we are or whether we can even get back on course to Mars. And those private tutors? How would she like asking a question and not getting the answer for 10 minutes? It's actually more like 20 minutes now, and 40 when we get to Mars, since radio waves travel at 300,000 kilometers per second. Talk about frustrating. Rory Galveston is pretty dreamy, but I've heard he's really stuck on himself, and he's way too old for me.*

"Larraine, can you help me with this history question?" Andrew interrupted her thoughts. "I don't get it."

"What's the question?"

"It's about the Civil War. I'm supposed to compare and contrast the North and the South. What's to compare? The North was in the north and the South was in the south."

"I think you're probably supposed to think about their reasons for going to war, the differences in their people and lifestyles, their advantages over each other, and their disadvantages."

"Well, yeah, but I don't understand all that stuff."

"Let's read about it first, and then I'll help you sort it out."

"It's a deal," Andrew smiled.

As Larraine and Andrew worked together on their studies, Damaris and Tony had their own problems with which to contend. Fortunately, the meteoroids had not damaged their ability to communicate with Earth, but the communication time delay between The Seeker and Mission Control was not helping the situation. It was taking a full 20 minutes to try something, report the results to Earth and then get a reply. The Seeker had been knocked slightly off course, and the longer it took to correct its trajectory, the more fuel it would take to make the correction. Fuel used now would deplete some of what they needed to be able to rendezvous with the Orbiter when they got to Mars. Damaris, Tony, and the mission controllers were all analyzing the problem so they could fix it with the least amount of fuel loss possible.

"Seeker, this is Mission Control. We have your coordinates, and we've determined what you need to do to get back on course. We've sent you the insertion burn sequence you need to follow by computer. We want you to follow our directions exactly, and then report back to us what your instruments are telling you. Then we'll be able to determine whether or not you are back on the Mars trajectory."

Damaris and Tony were both extremely tense. They knew that if this did not work, they would probably not have fuel enough to try another burn. The Seeker did not have storage space for large amounts of fuel. The fuel allowance was very thrifty—only what was absolutely necessary—plus just a little extra for an emergency like this. The Seeker was dependent on the influence of the Sun's gravity, coasting to Mars along an exact orbit. They knew they were off of that exact orbit. They needed to get back on track, at the exact speed, to stay in orbit around the Sun until they ran into Mars. As the data appeared on the computer screen, Damaris began inputting the coordinates while Tony readied to turn on the engines. They would fire the engines for 11 seconds to get back on course. Then the engines would require burning another 6 seconds to get them back to the correct orbital speed. This would require exactitude to the nth degree. Tony contacted Scott and Preston. "Are you guys about finished? As soon as you are back inside, we can light the engines and get back on course."

"We're getting ready to enter the airlock right now," answered Scott. "We've completed the repairs. Fortunately, nothing made it through the inner wall of the hull. Things are looking better."

"Great. Let us know when you are both inside. We have to light this candle as soon as possible." It seemed strange to see "Tiny Tony" so serious, as he usually had jokes to keep everyone laughing. In his late thirties, with brown, wavy hair, the Canadian was not much taller than Andrew.

Damaris closed her hazel eyes, mouthed a quick prayer, and opened the communication link to the lounge. "Larraine and Andrew, strap yourselves in. We're going to be turning the engines on for a short time." She shrugged her shoulders to loosen their tenseness, and shook her light brown hair. The dimpled, upturned corners of her mouth gave her a look of hope even in strained conditions like this.

The two children did as they were told. Even though both wanted reassurance from their mother, they realized that she did not have time to give it right now. During all their simulations on Earth they had learned to never question orders. Their lives could literally depend on following directions.

As soon as Scott and Preston were inside, Tony turned on the engines. The Seeker shuddered and pitched, but after weathering the meteoroids, this seemed like nothing. Damaris timed the burn, and Tony shut down the engines after exactly 11 seconds.

The tense atmosphere inside The Seeker was thick enough to cut with scissors as Tony asked, "Ready for the second burn?"

"Go for it," answered Damaris. She carefully timed for

the required 6 seconds, and then Tony shut the engines down. Now they just had to wait to hear from Mission Control. Were they back on a correct route to Mars, or would they die as they used up their air, orbiting the Sun forever, never to reach their destination?

CHAPTER 5

ANXIETY

At the same time on Mars:

The storm was getting worse. The dust was swirling, darkening the sky with an eerie brown-orange tint. The fines crackled against her helmet, and she imagined they were trying to penetrate it. She could no longer see into the distance, and the habitats of Terra Nova were becoming obscure. Could she make it to shelter? Dieffenbachia Bateman was terrified as she tried to run in the cumbersome spacesuit and tripped on an unseen rock. She began to hyperventilate as she felt her suit start to depressurize through a hole torn in the knee. "Please, God, help me," she screamed as she began to lose consciousness. *How ironic,* she thought. *I don't even believe in God.*

"Diff, wake up." Sandy's voice seemed to come out of nowhere. "You're having that nightmare again."

Dieffenbachia's dark green eyes sprang open, and she groped for Sandy in the dark. *Where am I?* Diff had only returned to Terra Nova from three months of duty aboard Hope two sols previously, and she was still in that hazy stage existing somewhere between sleep and reality. As her mind sharpened, she realized she was in her bunk inside the habitat she shared with Sandy Maloney, Sally Evanoff, Sachiko Tatsuda, and sometimes Jenny Colfax. Her heart had been charging like a locomotive, and it was beginning to stabilize once again. The cool air inside the pod chilled her as it surrounded her perspiring body. "Sandy," she whispered, "are you there?"

The light coming in through the pod's only porthole silhouetted Sandy Maloney's form as she quickly moved across the short space between her bunk and Dieffenbachia's. "I'm right here, Diff. Everything is okay."

Dieffenbachia took a deep, cleansing breath. "Thanks Sandy, for being there. That nightmare just won't leave me alone. It is so real."

"It's just a dream, Diff," Sandy reassured her. "Dreams aren't real, and they can't harm you."

"I know, but when the dream is happening, I just believe it. It's really scaring me. How am I going to be able to do my job around here? The dream never leaves me alone. I can't get it out of my mind."

"Why won't you pray with me about it?" asked Sandy.

"I don't believe in prayer. I don't believe in God. So how will that help me?" Dieffenbachia sat up straight and stiffened her shoulders.

"What's going on you two?" A weary voice wafted from across the hab. "It's the middle of the night, and we all have a busy sol tomorrow." Sally Evanoff's tousled blonde head peered from her bunk. She had barely turned in. Being second in command of Terra Nova had kept her up past two in the morning. Her pretty blue eyes were shrouded with sleep, and her usual optimistic attitude seemed non-existent at the moment.

"I had a nightmare," Dieffenbachia replied. "I'm not going to be able to sleep for awhile, so I'll go to the cafeteria. Sorry I woke you."

"Are you okay?" Sally was now concerned.

"I'll be fine. Go back to sleep." Dieffenbachia quickly threw on her neon green jumpsuit and headed for the door.

"Do you want company?" questioned Sandy.

"No thanks. I could use some time by myself. Thanks for offering, though."

The young pilot and engineer walked softly through the vinyl passageway from her pod to the cafeteria. *I hope I don't awaken anyone else,* she thought to herself. *It's already embarrassing enough. What is going on inside my head? This nightmare keeps terrorizing me. I can't get it out of my mind. What will Rod do if he finds out?*

Dieffenbachia Bateman, at the age of 33, had everything going for her. Barely a meter and a half tall, she was stunningly beautiful, attracting attention—both wanted and unwanted—wherever she was. Shoulder length, flaming red hair surrounded a face with high cheekbones and creamy white, flawless skin. Her dark green eyes, accentuated by the color of her jumpsuit, peered out from lush, black lashes. Not only beautiful, but smart and talented, she was used to getting whatever she wanted. As an Air Force ace pilot, she aspired to be an astronaut, and she made the cut with her first application. After an exhilarating NASA mission in orbit around Earth, she wanted Mars. In a short time, she had been selected and trained by UNSEF to pilot a spacecraft to the fourth planet. She had now been here for over a year and a half and was trying to decide whether she wanted to stay or return to Earth at the next opportunity.

Diff loved what she was doing; keeping a supply of oxygen continuously and flawlessly flowing on a planet having an atmosphere almost entirely composed of carbon dioxide was no simple matter. The entire settlement depended on her expertise, and that felt good. She also liked the solitude of Hope when she had her duty on the Orbiter. Her least favorite activity was working at the drilling site, but even that was an interesting, challenging, and important endeavor. *If it just wasn't for that nightmare!* Dieffenbachia had begun to think that there was something real to the dream. Why else would it keep returning, night after night? *I don't want to die on Mars,* she protested.

Why not? What do you have back on Earth? The cafeteria was thankfully empty, and Diff fixed herself a cup of coffee. *I really don't have anything back on Earth. I have no family, no pets, not even any real friends. Everyone I care about is here. Do I even care about anyone here? Well, I guess I care about Sandy. She's the closest thing I've ever had to a friend. I can tell she cares about me.*

Dieffenbachia Bateman had no known relatives. Her mother was an only child, and Diff's father deserted them when she was just a baby. Embittered, her mom never told Diff who he was. She had never known her grandparents, as they died before Diff was born. *My family seems destined to die young,* mused Dieffenbachia, as she remembered how her mother succumbed to a brain tumor shortly after Diff's selection for Officer Candidate School in the Air Force. Diff shuddered as her mind replayed the nightmare. *I wonder if it's a warning that I'm going to die early too?*

"Hey Diff, what are you doing up at this early hour? How do you stay so lovely with no beauty sleep?"

Dieffenbachia groaned inwardly. Pierre LaSalle, French engineer and ladies' man, was exactly the last person on Mars that she wanted to talk to right now. Pierre was tall with brown curly hair. His brown eyes were set inside dark, long lashes. He was quite good looking, and he knew it. He was used to having the ladies swoon over him, and Dieffenbachia was not cooperating. She had no interest in Pierre, which only seemed to make him more determined.

"Good morning, Pierre." Dieffenbachia's voice would have frozen liquid water if there had been any on the planet. "How is the drilling at Red City going?"

"Slowly, slowly," sighed Pierre. "We keep breaking drills, and since we can't order new ones, we must repair what we have. It seems like we spend more time repairing than drilling. We are all tired of looking at each other, and we are anxious for you to join us. When can we expect the pleasure of your company?"

A crew had been drilling at Red City for the past four years. Neutron spectrometer readings from Orbiters of the past had indicated the presence of large amounts of water below the surface of Mars. One of the expected sites was just 40 kilometers north of Terra Nova, so the drilling site was a natural extension of the base. Finding liquid water close to the established settlement was an UNSEF goal that would hasten its development and lead to more exploration and settlement of the planet.

Dieffenbachia knew she would be heading out for Red City soon. Jenny Colfax, Aaron Abrahamson, and Max Machiavelli were all due for some rest and relaxation at Terra Nova. Pierre was having his break now, which is why he was here. Diff suspected that Commander Rod Sherman would be sending her out to the remote location when Pierre went back out. She was not looking forward to it. She was unimpressed with Pierre's good looks, and his love of himself was a real turnoff. It also concerned her that he kept pursuing her.

"Rod hasn't told me when he wants me out there yet," replied Diff. "I'm not anxious to head out that way, as I just traded places with Brian on the Orbiter. Still, I know Jenny and Max need to come in."

"That's right," affirmed Pierre. "I have been telling the commander that he must send you out soon, so the rest of the Red City crew can have a break."

Dieffenbachia hoped that Pierre would move on, but he didn't.

"So," Pierre continued, digging for conversation, "you still have not answered my question. Why are you not sleeping? Why is such a beautiful woman up by herself in the middle of the night in the cafeteria?"

"Just couldn't sleep," answered Diff. with a yawn. "I'm starting to feel tired again now though. Maybe I'll try to go to sleep again."

"It is lovely out tonight. It's unusually clear and the

starry sky is incredible. Let's put on our spacesuits and go for a walk."

"No thank you, Pierre. I really must try to get some sleep now."

"You are breaking my heart, my Dieffenbachia," pleaded Pierre.

"Pierre, you know very well that isn't possible. Charm someone else."

Dieffenbachia put her cup into the microwave cleaner and beat a hasty exit back to her living quarters. *I hope I can sneak back into my bunk without waking up my roommates,* she thought. *Although, I doubt I can go back to sleep after running into Pierre. Dealing with him is more difficult than wrestling with the nightmare.*

CHAPTER 6

ORBITING MARS

Almost two months had passed since the nearly disastrous micro-meteoroid storm, and the vivid ocher sphere of Mars loomed before the viewing port, as Larraine and Andrew took turns gazing at it. Approaching Mars, the picture was diametrically different than the view observed while leaving Earth. Earth had been mostly blue, whereas there was certainly no blue to be found on this planet. Viewed from a distance, Earth gave the aura of peace, but the Romans and Greeks had long ago named the Red Planet for their god of war. The Romans called it Mars; the Greeks, Ares. Earth had prodigious cloud formations encircling it, while Mars presently had a few wispy, orange trails scudding across the hazy atmosphere. The dark side of Earth was adorned with scattered lights across its surface, but no such areas presented themselves on the Red Planet. And no continents emerged from the depths of the ocean on Mars. *How strange. No ocean.* "How can they possibly think we'll find life here?" Larraine asked no one in particular.

"What did you say?" Andrew briefly looked at his sister, and then returned his gaze to the awesome display before him.

"Oh nothing," sighed Larraine. "I just think it's a waste of time to look for life on a desolate, barren, totally dry world. Don't people think that life on Earth began in the water?"

"Mars isn't totally dry," argued Andrew, recalling his studies about the planet while back on Earth. "Mars has lots of frozen water in its ice caps, and they're even looking for water under the surface. There might be frozen water inside caves. And there is water vapor in its atmosphere. Besides all that, I think it's beautiful, so why shouldn't we find life on it?"

"I don't know about beautiful, but it certainly is amazing." Larraine, like Andrew, found it difficult to stop staring at the scene before her. It was like nothing she'd ever seen before. *All the pictures we saw, and all the studying we did, didn't prepare me for what I'm seeing now.*

The children could identify many of the distinctive Martian features—the Valles Marineris chasm, stretching more than 4,000 kilometers across the visible surface before them, and then the gigantic, 16-mile-high Olympus Mons, as large as the state of Arizona, dwarfing the west side of the Tharsis Bulge. They gazed on the ancient impact basins, the Argyre and Hellas Planitia. They tried to pick out Terra Nova, located just southeast of the Northern Ice Cap, nestled between the two ridges of the Chasma Boreale, but it was not distinguishable. It was difficult to believe that they were so close to Mars, after all the months of rocketing through empty (well, except for a few micro-meteoroids) space.

The journey was almost complete and the crew was noticeably upbeat. Captain Jamison, completely out of character, whistled a happy tune as he went about his duties. Tony Davis was checking and rechecking the trajectory data and planning the rendezvous with the Martian Orbiter, Hope. He was back to keeping things lively, joking and telling stories that amused the others. Preston Temple continued to spend several hours at a time in EVA gear, scouring the exterior of The Seeker to look for signs of meteoroid damage. No one was surprised that he found a few minor blemishes to repair. Damaris Temple was enjoying nearly instant communication with Brian Delaney, pilot and one of two people on-board the Orbiter. Delaney was obviously excited about The Seeker's arrival. It had been 2 months since he and Dmitri Nazarov had switched places on the orbiting habitat with Dieffenbachia Bateman and Chang Lee, and he was looking forward to hosting the weary travelers before their descent to the planet below.

Larraine found herself becoming excited about the mission, in spite of her misgivings. She would soon be living, learning, and exploring on a strange new world. Now that they were so close, she could hardly wait to step out onto the alien surface. She had seen pictures broadcast from Terra Nova, and she knew what the area would look like. Still, there was an unknown element. She already observed that pictures seldom do justice to the reality they portray. Pictures showed the Terra Novan cylindrical habitats growing from a rock strewn plain, punctuated by ridges along either side as far as one could see. Photos taken from the tops of the ridges showed an intricate network of strong, vinyl tunnels connecting modules that had been the supply containers for the first 6 arriving crews. The makeshift living quarters, called either pods or habs by the city's inhabitants, provided the only protection available to the settlers, and so far they were doing a good job. Since it was not affordable to ship construction materials from Earth yet, and Terra Novans had not yet begun manufacturing materials from the Martian natural resources, it looked as if the habs and their plastic connectors would have to do for now.

Four of the pods in the settlement were for living and sleeping—two for men, one for women, and the fourth for the first family. Larraine wondered how the rest of the crew there felt about that. *Would the family be welcomed or resented?* They had been true celebrities back on Earth, but she doubted that would be the case on Mars.

Set amid the living habs, there was a larger pod that had sections for eating and planning, as well as bathrooms containing showers. The communications center was also located in the heart of that pod. Upstairs, a loft provided a comfortable lounge area that the settlers prized. Attached to the front of the central pod was an airlock for entering the housing of the settlement.

A little to the east of the living habitat was the greenhouse, also attached to the central module by tubing. This allowed for pressurization inside the greenhouse, so work could be accomplished without spacesuits. It was easy to provide extra carbon dioxide for the plants from the Martian atmosphere, and still have breathable air for humans inside. The greenhouse was entirely constructed of clear, inflatable polymer to allow light from the sun to nourish the plants inside. Portable geodesic dome framing provided protection for the plasticized walls.

Last, but certainly not least in her brother's estimation, was the sixth pod or "shed" for the robots and rovers. The pod provided some protection from the Martian dust, but the mechanical contrivances obviously did not need pressurized areas like the people did. Andrew had read up on it, and knew that there were a variety of 'bots' on Mars. There were rovers for carrying equipment, transport vehicles for traveling and carrying gear long distances, and a few robots to help monitor conditions in the greenhouse and the production of water, oxygen, and fuel. He couldn't wait to actually see the mechanized equipment.

Construction in all areas was simple and scanty. The important thing was to keep people alive and in some degree of comfort, but no one had the time or materials available to make any of the living areas "homey." Larraine was pondering the bleakness of the two years stretching ahead of her and wondering if she would possess the determination and will to not just survive, but flourish. *"I can do everything through Him who gives me strength,"* she reminded herself.

"Seeker crew," Tony's jubilant voice wafted over the air. "We are 4 hours 6 minutes 32 seconds from rendezvous with the Orbiter, Hope. After seven months, are you tired of looking at just each other? Well, get ready. You are about to meet two new people! I'll let you know when you need to strap in."

When the Orbiter had first been planned, scientists felt

that it was time to put a positive satellite around Mars to offset the negative names long ago given its natural moons, Phobos and Deimos. Hence, it was given the name Hope. Hope had been circling Mars for ten years now, and it provided a much needed transition point for both arriving and departing crews.

The Seeker crew knew that Hope would be a welcome respite from the tiny spaceship that had transported them over the 400 million kilometers traveled between Earth and Mars. Its amenities included a small track that encircled the rest of the vessel, where a person could actually go for a decent walk or jog. They knew it was nothing fancy, but it would definitely be roomier than their present accommodations. Just knowing it would be different caused an undercurrent of excitement.

Six people living and working in the same small space-craft for seven months had been trying, to say the least. The fact that all were still on speaking terms spoke well for the group, but they were looking forward to some time away from each other. Docking with Hope would be a step closer to the time when they could feel solid ground under their feet once again.

Larraine and Andrew began making sure all of their meager belongings were accounted for, as they did not want to leave anything behind. The Seeker would not be taking them to the surface of Mars. It would stay attached to the Orbiter for the next six weeks, until a crew from Mars climbed aboard and took it back to Earth.

The Seeker crew would be transported to the planet on Hope's small shuttle. Larraine could hardly wait. She couldn't remember what standing on solid ground felt like. She knew it wouldn't be like Earth; Martian gravity was only about one third that of Earth, but she would still have something firm under her feet.

Larraine once again looked out of the porthole at the looming planet before her. *What will it really be like? Will I love it or hate it? Will people like us? Will it be totally incredible, or will I be bored out of my mind? What will there be for me to do, except study?* She sighed, putting away her troubled thoughts. Larraine knew it was time to embrace a new beginning, as she thought, *Ready or not, here I come.*

CHAPTER 7

MARS AT LAST!

It seemed as if only moments had passed, when the travelers gawked at a gigantic black wheel spinning around its central axis as it circled the planet below them. The Orbiter Hope loomed before them, presenting an awesome display of mankind's ingenuity. The spinning of the station was creating artificial gravity, pulling everything to its outer rim with centripetal force. Scott skillfully guided The Seeker to lock onto Hope's docking port. Once attached, huge doors automatically enclosed the spacecraft. The travelers disembarked inside an Orbiter airlock, after the chamber filled with air. Then its inner doors opened with a *whoosh,* and the crew of The Seeker looked into the attached Orbiter with anticipation. They were rewarded with the sight of two men, both dressed in vivid tangerine jumpsuits.

Brian Delaney's blue eyes sparkled in his beaming face as he saluted the crew and said, "Welcome aboard." Brian was lithe with curly, blond hair, and he loved being part of the Martian crew. He did admit to some loneliness during his tours aboard Hope, but he enjoyed the thrill of exploration and the camaraderie with the other Terra Nova citizens. As a pilot, he was often called on to transport others, sometimes between the planet and the Orbiter by shuttle, and sometimes in the large terra-rovers between Terra Nova and the remote drilling station. After spending the past two months aboard Hope with only Dmitri Nazarov, he was delighted to see the six members of The Seeker crew.

Standing right behind him was Dmitri, bouncing on the balls of his feet with anticipation. Dmitri's stay on Mars had taken its toll. A mechanical engineer from Russia, he had come to the fourth planet to work with the crew drilling for water northeast of Terra Nova. The drilling work was intense, and the drudgery had aged him tremendously, prematurely graying his hair, which gave him the appearance of being older than his forty-two years. In addition, every three months, he relieved Chang Lee on the Orbiter. Dmitri missed his family so much it hurt, and he hated the lonely vigil aboard Hope with Brian. He had a son Andrew's age and a daughter almost five now, and seeing the two children before him brought tears to his eyes. Dmitri was slated to head home on The Seeker in forty sols, when Earth, Venus, and Mars were lined up exactly right for the transfer, and he was more than ready.

Everyone began talking at once, in one giant ball of conversation and excited energy. Larraine and Andrew happily moved through the airlock door and into the Orbiter's spaciousness. It was heaven to peer into the corridor, which itself was wider than their Seeker sleeping quarters. "Mom, Dad, can I explore?" Andrew could hardly wait.

"I don't know," began Damaris.

"Of course, you may," replied Brian. "Just don't get lost."

Everyone smiled at the very idea, and Andrew danced down the corridor looking overhead into each opening. The walls on either side of the track held ladders for climbing into the rooms above and large viewing windows for observing as well. Andrew climbed the ladders, poking his head into every opening, and each seemed to expose something more incredible than the last. The group continued to hear his excitement. "Wow! It's an exercise room. Look at these bunks!" After five minutes, Andrew had made the entire circuit and was back to the others. He then realized that he had traversed a circular track just inside the outer rim of the Orbiter. The overhead openings led to the kitchen, sleeping areas, exercise room, control room, and lounge. All areas were larger than any of The Seeker's compartments, and Andrew was duly impressed. Larraine was somewhat jealous that she was 17 and was expected to act as an adult. If the truth was known, she wanted to take off and explore just like Andrew had. She firmed her jaw and prayed for patience, as she longed to take off and run on the track that circled the Orbiter. Continually spinning, the Orbiter created an artificial gravity like The Seeker's, but on Hope there was room to enjoy the pseudo-force.

Brian and Dmitri proudly showed the crew around the orbiting habitat. They enjoyed watching the expressions on each of the new arrivals' faces as they gazed on the remarkable facility. The last stop was at the kitchen, where the two had planned an extravagant meal.

Because of the Martian greenhouse, the explorers were able to enjoy fresh produce. The most successful plants grown were sweet potatoes, and it was amazing what a variety of dishes Sachiko Tatsuda, dietician and cook from Japan, had concocted from the versatile vegetable: baked, fried, boiled, or raw. Used in casseroles, salads, and even desserts, the sweet potato was never boring. Brian and Dmitri had brought freeze dried meals with them when they transported to the Orbiter, and they had outdone themselves in using the meals to prepare a welcome dinner.

The crew from Earth was impressed. Scott Jamison told them he had never had a steak as good as the sweet potato pie and legume salad they were devouring. Everyone marveled over the apple crisp for dessert, made with fruit from the bountiful harvest of trees planted twenty years ago by the first inhabitants from Earth. Even Andrew enjoyed the meal with nary a complaint about eating his vegetables.

The Seeker crew had a thousand questions about Terra Nova; questions about the people, the drilling, the latest discoveries, and the weather. They knew the names of the people stationed there, but very little else about them.

Dmitri began to fill the travelers in on the settlement. "Terra Nova is a harsh place. It is safe enough inside the habitats, but dangerous outside. You must, of course, wear a protective space suit any time that you go out. The Martian atmosphere doesn't provide enough oxygen for humans to breathe, and the atmospheric pressure is so low that without a pressurized suit, your blood would boil in less than two minutes."

"Gross," Andrew interjected. "Have you ever seen anyone's blood boil?"

"Certainly not," sniffed Dmitri, "and I hope I never do." He cocked his head and paused as if choosing his next words carefully; then continued, "Commander Sherman is a serious man with too much to do. He is tired and strict, and his rules seem harsh, but we all realize that those firm rules keep us safe, so we respect them. He has more knowledge and experience than anyone else. For many years he has overseen everything at Terra Nova as well as the remote drilling site."

"Remote drilling site!" exclaimed Andrew. "What are they drilling for, and can we go there?"

"They're drilling for water," Larraine indignantly replied, "and it isn't safe for us to go there."

"Since when have we been safe for the last seven months?"

"Andrew has a point," agreed Dmitri. "However, I am afraid that most settlers will not be allowed at the remote drilling site. Most wouldn't want to go. It is quite dangerous, and of course, isolated. There are usually only four people at a time out there."

"Don't they get scared and lonely out there?" asked Larraine.

"You bet they do," answered Brian. "They are very brave, and they persevere in hopes of making a difference. They know that their work has the potential to determine the future of the colony. It is the most important work being done on Mars."

"How do they stand being out there alone?" asked Tony.

"It's similar to spending time here on the Orbiter," replied Brian. "We start to really get stir crazy with just the two of us up here. That's why we rotate in and out with other people from Terra Nova. Dmitri and I have another month up here. Then we will be relieved by Dieffenbachia Bateman and Chang Lee. Diff gets the double whammy, just like Dmitri."

"What do you mean?" Damaris questioned.

"Diff is both a pilot and an engineer, and exceptional in both roles. She not only gets to spend three months at a time up here, in control of the Orbiter, but when she's on the surface of Mars, she goes out for two weeks at a time to give the remote crew some rest and relaxation back in Terra Nova."

"Isn't she afraid?" wondered Larraine.

"Nah," answered Brian. "She's as tough as any man on Mars, plus smarter and more skilled. I don't think she's ever afraid of anything."

"I can't wait to meet her," Larraine voiced dreamily. "She sounds very cool. I want to be like that."

Brian and Dmitri exchanged glances. "Well, I don't know about that," mused Dmitri. "She isn't very friendly. She does her job, but she doesn't want to have much to do with anyone else."

"Why not?" Andrew was perplexed. He thought Dieffenbachia Bateman sounded very interesting.

"I'll tell you why not," Scott's voice was gruff. "Diff has had a hard life. She's been on her own for a long time. No family and few friends. All she has is her work."

"Do you know Dieffenbachia?" Damaris expressed the surprise that all were feeling.

"I know her," Scott affirmed in a cheerless voice.

What's that about? thought Larraine. *I've never heard Scott sound sad. Angry yes, but sad? Not Scott.* However, she couldn't deny that his eyes looked unhappy and his thoughts seemed far away.

"Could we go to bed now?" Larraine found that being on Hope had given her body a relaxed feeling, and she was very sleepy.

"I think we could all use some shut-eye," affirmed Tony.

"Good idea," Dmitri agreed. "Brian and I take turns sleeping, but the rest of you should turn in. Tomorrow we'll transfer everything that needs to be taken to Mars into the shuttle and let you all get some exercise. Then the next sol, Sherman is expecting you to glide into Terra Nova."

———

The crew was strapped down in Hope's shuttle, excitedly waiting for the exact moment that they could release and plummet to the surface of Mars. They had spent 2 sols with Brian and Dmitri circling the planet in Hope. Only thirty minutes from their home of the next two years, they were more than ready. Each person privately considered the ramifications of what they had opted to do. If they were having second thoughts, it was too late now.

At the front of the shuttle were Scott, in the pilot's seat, and Tony beside him. Damaris and Preston sat next to each other in the middle, with Larraine and Andrew bringing up the rear. All were dressed in pressurized space suits, because they would need to deplane in the Martian atmosphere at the Terra Nova landing strip. Larraine and Andrew listened to Scott and Tony as they talked with both Hope and the ground crew. By releasing the shuttle at exactly the right moment and directing the shuttle into the Martian atmosphere, they would mostly glide their way to the surface. At some point, the children knew to expect a jolt as parachutes would be released to slow down their descent. Mars did not have a lot of atmosphere to help with the process, so the parachutes boasted a huge surface area—four times as large as that of the shuttle. They needed to create as much air resistance as possible in an atmosphere having one percent the pressure of Earth's. The shuttle would slow somewhat, and then Scott would direct it using the engines, into what they hoped would be a smooth and fast landing. Larraine breathed a prayer of thanks that they were riding with a world-class aerospace pilot.

Scott's voice sounded excited as he coordinated with the ground. "Mars Control, this is Hope Shuttle. We have input the insertion burn sequence, and we are standing by to release on your command."

"Hope Shuttle, this is Mars Control. We are at T-Minus 50 to release. All systems look good. We'll begin the count down at T-Minus 20 seconds."

"Roger that Mars Control." Scott turned to The Seeker crew, "Well, here we go guys and gals. Next stop—ready or not—Mars."

The countdown had begun. Larraine's pulse was blasting like a meteor. She took several deep breaths and silently prayed, trying to remind herself that this was much easier than traversing all the way from Earth to Mars. It wasn't working, however. Her imagination ran wild. *What if the insertion burn sequence isn't perfect? We'll bounce off the atmosphere of Mars and be thrown into outer space. What if the parachutes don't open? What if we don't slow down enough and the friction of the atmosphere burns us up? What if Scott overshoots the landing strip? Lord, protect us.*

"5 . . . 4 . . . 3 . . . 2 . . . 1 . . . Release!"

CHAPTER 8

LANDING

Within minutes, the thrilling ride ended as the shuttle landed roughly on the pebble-strewn runway outside of Terra Nova. Scott had done his job perfectly, steering the craft to a flawless touchdown. Finally, after seven months and 400 million kilometers, the crew was once again on firm ground. It was a weird but awesome feeling, to have solidity under them.

Larraine could see people in spacesuits waiting beside the runway to greet them, as well as the ground crew to help direct the shuttle now that it had landed. She counted five people in all; two were directing Scott and three others were standing by. Of course, all were in pressurized spacesuits, so it was impossible to tell who the five were. *I wonder who is going to greet us? Will the people here at Terra Nova be glad we came? Will they like us? Will I like them? What if we don't fit in?* Larraine was more than a little worried about their acceptance. How would the settlers feel about her and Andrew?

Scott had his own concerns about their arrival. *Where is Diff?* His mind returned to the last time he had seen her. It had been three years ago when they were both involved in astronaut training. From the first day they had met, they seemed like soul mates, and their relationship had grown from true friendship to a lot more. In fact, Scott knew that he had been in love with

Dieffenbachia. They had both applied for Mars, and were sure they would be picked for the next mission. After all, the two of them were at the top of the class. Then came the day when Diff was selected and Scott overlooked. That was the beginning of the end for the duo. Scott shuddered as he remembered how his jealousy had driven Diff away from him. He had never forgiven himself, but the damage was done.

Damaris had her own concerns. She had been briefed about Sammy's strange illness, and she hoped she would be able to quickly determine what his problem was. Then she hoped that she had what she needed to help him.

Preston was having misgivings about bringing his family to Mars. *What if they didn't survive this?* When they had been selected, he had been so sure, but he wasn't confident anymore. Although he had hidden his anxiety from the others, the meteoroid shower had shaken him far more than he let on. With a stronger hull penetration, they could have all been killed. *I'll never forgive myself if anything happens to my kids,* Pres told himself.

Tony and Andrew, however, were genuinely glad to be here. Both were experiencing elated thoughts of how incredible it was to actually be on another world. *I can't believe they picked me for this,* Tony mused. Andrew thought, *I can't get out of this shuttle fast enough. I wonder how soon I can go out exploring? How far will they let me go? Can I take a robot with me?*

Scott cautiously popped the hatch, gave a thumbs-up sign to his fellow crew members, and began to climb out of the shuttle. As his foot touched solid ground, he was overwhelmed. *I'm actually stepping on Martian soil. How incredible is that?* He was followed by Tony, then Damaris and Preston, with Larraine and Andrew close behind.

Awed as they scanned the panorama displayed before them, more than one of the travelers wished they could view it without the protective gear. Photographs had not prepared them for what their eyes beheld. The habitats of Terra Nova sprawled between the protective ridges of the Chasma Boreale, the glistening reddish walls towering to meet the hazy, pink Martian sky. There was nothing futuristic looking about the settlement; conversely, it was obviously utilitarian, planned thoughtfully to make use of available materials that were mostly former transport vehicles. Along with each former spacecraft to carry passengers, UNSEF had sent along supply containers that now served as the habitats.

It really is a frontier, Larraine marveled. *And now, we're part of it.*

The six fellow travelers began their trek across the runway to meet the greeting party. They were amazed at how easy their progress seemed, even inside the bulky pressurized suits, due to the fact that the Martian gravity was not as great as that they experienced artificially while traversing on The Seeker or orbiting on Hope. The revolving of those space craft had been planned to simulate an earth-like gravity. The gravity of Mars was only one-third as strong as the gravity of Earth. They all found that they were well prepared physically for walking on Mars, unlike the first travelers to Mars who had tried to keep their muscles strong by just exercising. After 7 months of microgravity, the muscles of the first astronauts had weakened in spite of their exercise regimen, and they had found the gravity of Mars to be very strong. Every step seemed as difficult as walking in thick mud. UNSEF had learned from the original crews that they needed to simulate gravity and not just depend on exercising.

As the three greeters stepped out to meet them, Andrew's feet became springs and he bounced up and down with anticipation. He easily jumped a half-meter high with each bound, and knew he already liked Mars. "Welcome to Terra Nova," laughed Rod Sherman's greeting. All could hear his voice, because of the radio receivers built into their headsets. "I am Commander Rod Sherman. I'm in charge of Terra Nova, and on behalf of the entire settlement, it is my honor to show you the habitats and your new home. Everyone is thrilled that you are here, and most will be making your acquaintance at dinner tonight. With me are Sally Evanoff, my second in command, and Rory Galveston, one of our geologists."

Scott saluted smartly and responded, "We are happy to be here, Commander, and we are ready to serve in whatever capacity you desire."

"No saluting is necessary at Terra Nova," Rod protested. "We're pretty casual up here. We'll let you all rest for a couple of sols, and then we'll discuss jobs and such." As an afterthought, he added, "That is, all but Dr. Temple. We need to have her to look in on Sammy Yoon as soon as she can."

"Of course," replied Damaris. "Why don't we go check him out right now?"

The two settlers who had directed the shuttle in busily unloaded it, putting everything on a terra-rover, a true Martian muscle machine. Terra-rovers were as big as tanks and could carry people and gear great distances. However, that's where the similarity ended. The terra-rovers were open-air transport vehicles and sported no weapons. The powerful machines had even dragged and pushed the pods of Terra Nova to their present positions from where they had landed nearby. While providing the much needed service of transporting heavy items, they were never anyone's choice to ride for short distances.

"We have everything loaded, Rod. Are you all ready to climb aboard so we can get back to the habs?" asked the short, chubby Chang Lee. "Or would you prefer to walk?"

"Let's ride," answered Rod. "Our new inhabitants should definitely experience a terra-rover." The commander turned to the new arrivals. "Seeker crew, this is Chang Lee and Pavel Stanislof, but you won't recognize any of us until we get back inside and can remove our space suits."

Wrong, smiled Larraine. *I'll always recognize Chang by his shape.* Then she chastised herself, knowing she wouldn't want the rotund mechanical engineer to overhear her thoughts.

"This transportation isn't like what you're used to on

Earth," warned Chang, with a smile in his voice. "It's primitive and slow. It helpfully carries gear for us, and luckily, we don't have far to go. Climb on and hold on. We don't want to lose anyone."

I like him already, Larraine thought.

Andrew nearly bounced into the vehicle, and all could hear his giggle as he settled in. The rest approached more carefully, but just as eagerly. Pavel hefted himself into the driver's seat, turned on the rover, and put it in gear. The crew found that Chang had not exaggerated when he said the ride would be rough. The violent vibrations knocked them into each other unforgivingly. Eight huge wheels of solid metal encased in rubberized vinyl lumbered over rocks of all sizes as the vehicle took on everything in its way. Built to last, comfort was not a consideration when the transport was designed. Only Andrew seemed unaffected by the constant jostling as they made their way to the settlement before them.

"How fast does this thing go?" laughed Tony.

"About five kilometers an hour," answered Chang. "We could walk faster, but this is a good way to lose weight."

Even Andrew was glad to get off the transport as they parked next to the settlement. The new members of the base all gazed at the establishment in wonder. Close up, it was even more amazing. For one thing, the pods were taller than they had seemed from a distance. The habs sprawled against a backdrop of red, rocky wall and were interconnected haphazardly with heavy vinyl tubing. It wasn't pretty, but seemed efficient. The central pod appeared to have a porch reaching out in front to welcome visitors.

As The Seeker crew stared, Rod explained, "That's our airlock. We'll all enter into it four at a time and close the door. Then there's a second door inside leading to the interior of the central pod. We open that door only after the first door is fully closed. That way, we keep our air in and the Martian atmosphere out. Once inside, you can all remove your space suits, and you'll be protected by the hab's exterior. We have a pressurized, oxygen-rich atmosphere inside, with a comfortable temperature. It will seem just like home."

I seriously doubt that, objected Larraine to herself. *Andrew and I called The Seeker airlock a tin can, but it looks to me like we'll be living for the next two years inside a real tin can.*

Rod led the way into the airlock. It took awhile to move everyone indoors, as four filled the space to capacity. Since Larraine and Andrew were the youngest, they were escorted through first with Rod and Rory. They began removing their protective gear as the others took turns getting in. It was a slow process, and Larraine wondered what would happen if a number of inhabitants ever had to hurriedly move inside. *What if there was a huge emergency, and everyone had to take cover, like really fast?*

Inside the hab and to the left, there was a storage area for hanging the protective gear. Just past it were bathrooms. Looking around, the new inhabitants could see the cafeteria and a communications station. Just off of the cafeteria, they saw a ladder attached to the wall, leading to an upper level. They also noticed five tunnel-like holes, which they imagined led to the living and sleeping habs and the greenhouse. It was obvious that everything had been carefully laid out, and every centimeter of space had been used, in spite of the chaotic appearance from the outside.

"What's behind that?" asked Andrew, noticing a curtained off area directly in front of the airlock.

"That's Sammy Yoon's hospital room," answered Rory. "We had to move him off by himself in case he has something contagious."

"Has anyone else had symptoms like his?" questioned Damaris.

"No," replied Rory, "and he's been really sick for two months."

"How long was he sick before you separated him?"

"That's hard to say. He hasn't been feeling well for a long time," stated Rory. "It seems like he was really sick about a week before we confined him."

Damaris thought before she spoke. "I don't think anyone will catch what he has. If he was sick for a week, you were all exposed to whatever it is. Also, you don't exactly have an isolated area there. So if what he has is contagious, more people should have it by now."

"You're probably right," admitted Rod, "but we tried to be careful. We don't really have a way to isolate anyone completely."

"Could you take us to our living quarters and give me a few minutes to find my medical supplies? Then I'd like to examine Sammy and get him moved back in with the other men. I think he'd be more comfortable and a lot happier."

Rory smiled. *This doctor might just be the best thing that's happened around here for awhile.*

CHAPTER 9

EXAMINATION

"So when did you first start to feel sick?" Damaris had just finished checking Sammy's pulse and blood pressure. She looked compassionately at his sunken, dark-circled eyes and skeletal appearance. The once healthy, muscular body was clearly wasting away.

"Well, I noticed that I couldn't breathe very well right after we got to Mars and started living in the pods. I was just a little short of breath—nothing serious—so I didn't pay much attention to it."

"Sammy, any time you are short of breath, you should pay attention to it. Your body can't function properly if it isn't getting enough oxygen. In fact, your body can only last about 5 minutes without oxygen. All of your cells need it. Why don't you fill me in on how this illness progressed."

"Well, as I said, I first started feeling short of breath," recalled Sammy. "That went on for quite awhile. Gradually, I started feeling weak and coughing a lot. I was still going out exploring with Rory, and I would feel better when I was out away from the settlement. But then we'd come back, and my body would feel so fatigued, I could hardly stand."

"You said you noticed being short of breath right after you arrived and began living in the pods," restated Damaris.

"Do you mean to tell me this has been going on for almost two years?"

"Only one Martian year, Doctor," joked Sammy.

"I'm serious Sammy," Damaris scolded. "It's a wonder you're still as healthy as you are. How long have you been bed-ridden?"

"About 2 months," Sammy admitted.

"Have you ever had allergies or asthma?"

Sammy thought a moment. "When I was a kid, I was pretty allergic to cats and dust. I outgrew it, though."

"Maybe, and maybe not," thought Damaris aloud.

"What do you mean? Do you think I'm allergic to something in here?" Sammy was incredulous. "How can that be? We are totally sealed up and only breathing oxygen-rich air. And I did fine on the same air all the way to Mars in the spaceship." A fit of coughing caused Sammy to lie back down, helplessly. His chest heaved up and down as the coughs controlled his entire being. He gasped for breath and groaned between spasms.

"Sammy, I want you to rest and not talk now. I'm going to take a sample of your blood for analysis. I'm not sure it's going to tell me much, but at least I can use it to eliminate some things." Damaris posed a question. "How would you feel about moving back into the hab with the other guys?"

"Are—you—serious?" Sammy choked. "Will they—be okay with—that?"

"They will when I tell them you don't have anything contagious."

"Are you—sure—about that?" Sammy sounded hopeful.

"I'm almost positive. I just have a few tests to run on you, but I think we can have you back in your room in a couple of sols. That doesn't mean you'll feel better, however."

"I'll feel—better, all right," argued the geologist. "It's horrible—spending every sol—alone behind this curtain, out in the middle—of everything, yet away from—everyone."

70

"Okay, Sammy. I'll do my best to get you back into your hab as soon as possible," Damaris promised. "You'll still need to be in bed for the time being, but at least you'll have people to talk with."

"Thanks, Doc."

"You rest now, Sammy."

"That's all I do, Doctor Temple. I'm—tired—of resting. Could you bring me—the computer assigned—to geology? I'd like to do some research—to help Rory out—with the specimen he brought in from the cave."

"I'll see if it can be arranged. But you have to promise that you won't overdo it. I know you don't want to admit it, but your body is frail and weak right now."

Damaris took Sammy's blood sample to the Temple hab, where she had equipment for studying it. Then she decided to take a look around. She believed that Sammy was showing clear signs of severe asthma induced by an allergic reaction to something, but what could it be? Sammy was right that the pods were sealed and pressurized, so human bodies could walk around comfortably without bulky spacesuits while inside. As far as she could tell, the enclosures seemed almost as spotless as a clean room back at NASA.

Damaris looked first in the small cafeteria area. Could Sammy be having a reaction to any of the fresh vegetables that were grown in the greenhouse? She would have to ask him if he had ever had problems with sweet potatoes, peas, or beans, but knew it wasn't likely.

She found Tony at work in the communications area. He had begun performing a critical job in this area almost immediately. Rod had been hoping to establish a full-time link with Earth, but had not had the personnel necessary to do this before the arrival of The Seeker crew. Tony was experienced with communications, and he was one of the few who were not exasperated with the 40-minute time delay in getting responses from Earth. Tony had been assigned a 10-hour shift, with the remaining hours of the sol divided into 2-hour increments to be filled by other explorers. Everyone in Terra Nova would be expected to take a shift on a rotating basis.

"You look satisfied, Tony," observed Damaris.

"I am," Tony affirmed. "This is my calling. It's the most important job at this base, and I am just the man for the job."

"There are others who might argue with you about that," Damaris smiled. "About it being the most important job on the base."

"You just wait," Tony protested. "Wait until the first emergency."

"I can do without emergencies."

"You wish. So how is the patient?"

"I'm really concerned about him," Damaris worried. "He is very sick. He's showing classic signs of severe asthma, possibly triggered by an allergic reaction, but I can't imagine what he could be having trouble with in this environment."

"Good luck."

"Yeah, thanks."

Damaris continued looking through the main hab. It all seemed so spotless, but she knew that some things are too small to be seen by human eyes. She turned and looked at the airlock. *Now what is that?* The floor near the door was smudged with a reddish brown color. Looking closer, she noticed tiny fragments of Martian soil all around the airlock door as far as the storage area. She opened a door and looked closely at the space suit inside. The boots and bottom of the suit were covered with fine, reddish dust. *Could Sammy be allergic to Martian dust? Every time someone comes in from the outside, they inadvertently bring some in with them. If he is, his present location is the worst possible place for him to be. He's in very close proximity to all of this dust.*

Damaris made a split second decision. *Sammy's going back to his hab right now!*

CHAPTER 10

SETTLING IN

During her first week on Mars, Larraine turned on her handheld computer, plugged in its keyboard, and began composing a letter to transmit back to Earth. It had been several weeks since she had written to Lucy and Marta, and she had so much to tell them. *Where do I begin?* Her hands quickly moved over the keyboard as she composed her thoughts.

Solaris 5, 2045

Dear Lucy and Marta,

I am sending this to Lucy, and I'm depending on you, Lucy, to share it with Marta. Next time, I'll send the letter to Marta.

After 200 days of traveling faster than a speeding bullet and experiencing everything from unending and unbearable boredom to sheer terror, we are at last here on Mars in Terra Nova.

Take a look at the date of my letter. We go by a Martian calendar up here. Earth's doesn't really work, because on Mars, a year is almost twice as long as a year on Earth. So we have a 23-month calendar. You see, a year on Mars has 687 sols, whereas Earth's year has 365 days. We have 22 months, each 30 sols long, and a short 27 sol month to complete our year. Now you do the math and see if that adds up! It's too confusing for me to get it straight. I'm copying it off of some information they gave us when we arrived.

Anyway, we are now in the 14ᵗʰ month of the Martian trip around the sun, and it is Solaris. Since the years don't really work with Earth's, we're continuing to measure time by Earth years–thank goodness! So the month is for Mars, but the 2045 reflects the year on Earth and Mars.

If that isn't confusing enough, think about clock time here. A Martian sol is 39.5 minutes longer than an Earth day. We still have a 24-hour clock though. Scientists have mathematically figured out 24 Martian hours. Those are each divided into 60 Martian minutes, which are divided into 60 Martian seconds. Obviously, Martian seconds are a little longer than Earth seconds. Believe it or not, it seems to work. For years my mom has said she wishes she could have more time in the day. Well, now she does!

I almost forgot. A Martian day is not called a day. It's called a sol. So instead of daybreak, we have solbreak, and rather than daytime, it's soltime. Daylight is sollight. Will I ever get used to that?

You'll be interested in this. Guess what the fashion is here in Terra Nova. We all have been issued regulation coveralls in the weirdest colors you can imagine. Someone, somewhere, decided that bright colors would help balance the lack of artistic amenities here. My outfit is hot pink. Can you imagine me in hot pink? It is just the worst. Maybe not–Andrew's is canary yellow. My mom and dad both lucked out with a brilliant blue of some kind.

It is winter here now. The seasons last twice as long as they do on Earth, so imagine six months of winter. Of course we always wear protective suits outside, so our bodies don't really notice a temperature difference. It's always cold on Mars, no matter what season it is. The temperature is almost always below freezing. Right now, the ground is often covered with a light dusting of frozen carbon dioxide ice, which is very pretty.

I was so excited to finally get here, and I was looking forward to having some privacy after the cramped quarters of The Seeker. Wrong! Now I'm sharing a large two-story can with my whole, entire family. Can you even begin to imagine? And I think we have more room than most of the others here. In fact, I can tell that some people are slightly ticked because of it. They think we are being given special treatment, which may be true—I don't know.

Most of the people are glad we're here though, especially because now they have a real doctor in the settlement after two years without one. People alternate with others out at the remote drilling site 40 kilometers from Terra Nova every two weeks, and my dad's going to be heading out eventually. I don't like it; can't help worrying about him going out there away from us, but it will just be for two weeks at a time.

Tony went to work on communications right away, but he'll take turns on Hope with Scott every three months. They even have things for Andrew and me to do. Andrew thinks he is in Martian heaven. When he finishes his homework, he gets to spend time with Pavel Stanislof, the Russian mechanical engineer who is in charge of the rovers and robots. Pavel is teaching Andrew all about them and how they work, including how to repair them. Talk about motivation! No one has to tell Andrew twice to do his homework.

As for homework, I am really loaded. It's all interesting and challenging, so I shouldn't complain. Lucy, you will be so envious when I tell you that I am studying some geology with Rory Galveston. You are so right that he is gorgeous–lots better looking than his pictures. Beyond that, I'm not sure what to think of him. He's certainly not thrilled to be teaching me. I'm also studying calculus with my dad, literature with my mom, and botany with Sandy Maloney. She and Hiro Tatsuda from Japan are in charge of the greenhouse here, and it's so cool to see what they

75

have growing right here on planet Mars. You wouldn't believe it. There are all kinds of vegetables—sweet potatoes, corn, beans, and peas. Fruit trees were planted by some of the first settlers 20 years ago, and they are producing tons of apples, peaches, and oranges.

There is also a huge fish tank located in the greenhouse to hold hundreds of tilapia fish. These fish lay and fertilize tons of eggs that hatch and grow fast. It's a good thing they reproduce quickly, because we eat the fish frequently. They are a great source of protein and pretty tasty too. We also even have a colony of bees inside the greenhouse that pollinate plants and make honey. Pretty amazing, right? I'm glad I wasn't on the spaceship that brought that to Mars!

In addition to homework, I'm supposed to help in the greenhouse for 2 hours a sol (that's a Martian day, remember?) tending the plants. I've been learning about the watering and fertilizing needs of the different kinds of plants, as well as replanting, and thinning. It's interesting and also important work for our survival, so I don't mind really.

Of course, more than seven months have passed since we have been to church. I know that God has been with us on our journey, but I sure do miss church and the youth group. My dad plans to hold a Sunday (I wonder if that should be Sunsol?) worship service upstairs in the lounge area of the main hab for anyone who wants to come. When he told Commander Rod Sherman, he seemed surprised but open to it. I wonder who will show up?

Did you ever wonder how in the world (or should I say how in Mars?) we get enough oxygen for all of us on this planet? You know, there isn't much in the atmosphere here. And since a person can only last about 5 minutes without oxygen, having enough is pretty important. I guess you could say it's vital. Dieffenbachia Bateman (you know who she is, right?) showed us the life support recycling center. That's right—it's a recycling system. It is truly amazing. I don't understand the chemistry yet, but it seems to work. The first settlers brought a lot of hydrogen with them, and part of their landing craft was a chemical processing unit that draws in carbon dioxide from the Martian atmosphere, somehow combines it with the hydrogen, and that combination produces methane and water. The methane is stored to mix with oxygen for fuel. Every time the shuttle makes a trip to Hope, it uses the manufactured fuel. The shuttle also carries some fuel to the Orbiter where it is stored in holding tanks for the Orbiter's use and for refueling spacecraft returning to Earth.

The precious water produced is also saved, and some of it is used for drinking, cleaning, and for watering the plants in the greenhouse. The rest is split into its elements—hydrogen and oxygen. Some of the oxygen is stored for fuel, but most of it is piped to the habs and stored in containers for us to breathe, and the hydrogen is used to make more water and methane using the Martian carbon dioxide. As I said—a recycling center. Since the Martian atmosphere is 95 percent carbon dioxide, there is no danger of running out. And we have two of these recycling centers in case anything goes wrong with one of them.

Dieffenbachia Bateman is awesome. She's beautiful and smart, and she is eventually supposed to teach me some chemistry. I don't know when that will happen, though, because she is slated to leave this week for the remote drilling site. She'll be out there for two weeks, and then she's supposed to take over on the Orbiter Hope, for 3 months, unless she pilots The Seeker back to Earth. I wish I could go there with her. She is amazing, and I'd like to work with her and get to know her better. I wish I looked like her. She's tiny! Let me tell you, she is definitely a distraction to all the men who see her. I think she and Scott must have some sort of history, because they totally avoided each other when she was showing us around. She didn't look at him or talk to him or anything, but she didn't treat the rest of us like that. I felt sorry for Scott, because I caught him peeking at her guardedly when he thought she wasn't looking. I wonder what's going on there.

Mars isn't really what I expected. For instance, we've all learned that it is red because of the rusted iron in its soil. That's true, but when you are here looking around, the rocks are mostly gray in color. It's just that the dust (it isn't really dust like we think of dust) that covers everything is the reddish color. The particles of dust are technically called fines. The fines are everywhere and get into everything. They are so fine, they float around in the air, causing a constant haze, so the sky looks pinkish almost all the time. My mom thinks Sammy Yoon might be allergic to the fines, so she is sending him to Hope with Dieffenbachia Bateman when she goes. I hope he improves up there, because his body doesn't look like it can last much longer if something doesn't change.

Being on a new world has shown me tons more of the creative genius of God. It is so different from Earth, yet incredibly beautiful and wonderful in its own way. But I don't think we'll find any evidence of life here. I think God put life on Earth and probably not anywhere else.

Gotta run to the greenhouse, so I'm going to close this for now. The week ahead looks good. Andrew and I get to go on an off-site geology trip with Rory Galveston. How about that?! Write back soon. I miss you all so much.

Love,
Larraine

Larraine took the computer to Tony in the communications center for help with transmitting and hoped to hear from her friends soon. The thought of being the only 17-year-old for at least 150 million kilometers depressed her. Larraine gritted her teeth, remembering that they had traveled 400 million kilometers orbiting the Sun in order to get to a planet that was usually only one third as far as that away from Earth. Taking a deep breath, she determined to learn all she could, stay busy every waking minute, and return to Earth in two years, regardless of what the rest of her family chose to do.

Later that sol, Larraine worked in the greenhouse with

Sandy Maloney and Hiro Tatsuda. Sandy oversaw everything about the greenhouse, and Hiro assisted her. Big changes were about to take place, because Sandy was slated to return to Earth when The Seeker left. That meant Hiro would be taking over, and he needed assistance.

From Japan, Hiro had joined his twin sister Sachiko on Mars two years ago along with Sandy, Brian Delaney, and Rory Galveston. Both Tatsudas were small with dark hair and eyes. They were strikingly good looking and resembled each other. Sachiko was the only adult at Terra Nova who was smaller than Dieffenbachia Bateman, and Hiro was barely taller than she.

As Sandy watched and listened, Hiro demonstrated and taught. "The atmosphere on Mars is perfect for plant life," he told Larraine. "The plants thrive on the extra carbon dioxide. Even though we bring oxygen into the conservatory right now for our needs, the air in here has much more carbon dioxide than the air on Earth. So as long as we monitor the temperature carefully and water each species accurately, the plants will flourish. We've already proven that."

Sandy interrupted Hiro's lecture. "Since plants transpire oxygen, we hope the greenhouse will eventually support our breathing needs without help from the recycling center."

Surprised, Larraine asked, "Do you think that's really possible?"

"We sure do," responded Hiro. "There've been many studies done back on Earth showing that it's possible. The idea is one of the foundations of terraforming. Although it would take thousands of years, theoretically we should be able to eventually warm the Martian surface, and that would allow a thicker atmosphere and foster greater atmospheric pressure. Then by encouraging abundant plant growth across the surface of Mars, we could begin to oxygenate that atmosphere. Ultimately, Mars could be changed into a warm, moist planet more like Earth. Mars could be terraformed."

"Wow!" the teen-ager exclaimed. "I had no idea."

Sandy smiled and continued. "So you see, we not only have the responsibility of keeping everyone fed, but we hope to provide a source of oxygen some sol as well."

Larraine looked around at the prolific life—everything from fruit trees to vegetables growing under the soil—and she felt proud to be part of the endeavor. "I'm really glad to help you two out here, but I am a little worried. I don't know much about plants, and the greenhouse is so important."

"Don't be concerned," Hiro assured her. "We can teach you everything you need to know. I'll miss Sandy's expertise, but I'm not exactly a novice as far as plants go. I know what they need, and I'll be in charge. We won't ask you to do anything unless we prepare you for it."

"That's right," agreed Sandy. "It has been great for both Hiro and I to work together on this project, but either one of us could have done it with just the help of trainees. Now both of us have a few weeks to train you. We know you will be a great help."

Larraine sincerely hoped so. Never having felt such responsibility before, she promised herself that she would not let them down. She would earnestly do her best and rely on God to help her. Larraine smiled at Sandy and Hiro, took a deep breath, and said, "I'm ready and willing to learn. Teach me everything you can."

CHAPTER 11

THE DIAGNOSIS

Later that week, Dr. Temple argued with Sammy about her decision.

"But Doc," protested Sammy, "I have so much work to do here."

"You're not going to be able to accomplish much in bed, Sammy," Damaris argued. "I want you to spend some time on Hope and just see if it makes a difference. I think you are having an allergic reaction to the Martian fines. There is no way to keep them completely out of the habs, but on the Orbiter, you won't be exposed to them at all."

"What if I get up there and I don't get better? Or even get worse? What then?"

Damaris sighed. "I don't know, Sammy, but we have to try it. We all want you to get better."

"She's right about that," came Rory's voice from behind Damaris. She turned to see him looking at Sammy with great concern. "I'll miss you, you old prospector, but you need to get well."

"Listen to Dr. Galveston, Sammy." Damaris welcomed Rory's support. "He knows what he's talking about."

"Can't I at least go out to the cave one time?" Sammy's immense disappointment was evident.

"Oh sure, Sammy. We'll just load you onto a rover and your teeth can rattle all the way out there," joked Rory.

Sammy's eyes clouded over as he tried to smile back. "I've come all this way, all for nothing. What a failure I've been."

"Wrong!" insisted Rory. "Whose idea was it for us to explore south of Terra Nova, and who discovered the washout area? It was you. I would have never found the cave if you hadn't found the washout. You can still help me out from Hope by researching and analyzing the data that I can send you. We're a team, and I'm not letting you quit yet."

"Rory, you know they'll send me home when The Seeker leaves. This opportunity is over for me." Sammy's voice was resigned.

Damaris met Rory's eyes as she moved to the other side of Sammy's cot. She began to take his pulse as she tried to change the subject. "So how is it being back with the guys?"

"All the snoring keeps me awake," complained Sammy.

"Do you want me to put you back where you were?" teased Damaris.

"No, that's okay," Sammy quickly responded. "I'll get used to it."

"I don't know how you can complain," Rory argued. "You're a chainsaw when you sleep."

"Well, keep an eye on him, Rory. Take it easy, Sammy. I'll be back to check on you later. In the meantime, I'm going to book your reservation on the next shuttle to Hope."

The end of the first week on Mars found Larraine softly singing a song of praise, as she was replanting some pea seedlings in the greenhouse. Suddenly aware of someone watching her, she self-consciously stopped and looked up into the vibrant, smiling green eyes of Dieffenbachia Bateman.

"You've got a great voice," commented Diff.

"Sorry," Larraine apologized. "I sometimes sing while I work. I didn't know anyone else was in here."

"I was looking for you, Larraine. I'm being sent out to the remote drilling site for the next two weeks. I leave tomorrow morning, and after the stint at the drilling site, I will have a few sols here, and then I'll be relieving Brian Delaney in the Orbiter. I am looking forward to working with you, but I don't know when we'll be able to get together."

Larraine was bummed and tried unsuccessfully not to show it. Noticing the girl's disappointment, Diff continued, "Maybe they'll let you come spend some time on Hope with me. I will have quite a bit of time on my hands up there."

"That would be great." Larraine perked up.

"Do you have a few minutes now?" asked Diff. "I'd like a cup of coffee, and we could sit and get acquainted a little."

"Just let me finish watering these plants, and I'll be right there." Larraine could hardly believe it. *I thought she was supposed to be unfriendly, and here she is, inviting me to get acquainted.* Larraine hurriedly watered the plants so she could meet with Dieffenbachia in the cafeteria. She had wanted to hang out with Diff ever since The Seeker crew's arrival. This was her chance.

Diff had already poured her coffee and she was reading something as Larraine shyly approached. Looking up, the older woman smiled. "That was quick. What would you like to drink? Grab it and join me."

Larraine went to the refrigeration unit and poured herself some juice. Sachiko had created a vegetable and fruit concoction from the produce being grown in the greenhouse, and the girl had found that it was pretty decent. Taking a sip, she tried to imagine what was in the drink. She could clearly taste apple and sweet potato, but beyond that, it was hard to say.

Sitting down, she tried to think of something intelligent to say. "Why do you have to go out to the drilling site? Why can't someone else do it?"

Diff shrugged her shoulders. "Who would you send in my place?"

"I don't know, but it doesn't seem fair that you have to drill and also go pilot the Orbiter. That's a lot for one person."

"Larraine, each person sent here has a big responsibility, and each one was carefully chosen because of his or her specific training and skills. I was chosen over others because I am both a good pilot and a good engineer. I knew when I came to Terra Nova that it would be hard work and that I would need to help out in both places."

"But we need your engineering skills here too. I know you help keep the life support recycling center running. What could be more important than that?"

Diff sighed. "You're right about that, but that's also Rod Sherman's responsibility. And your dad has had training to help with that as well. Max Machiavelli and Jenny Colfax, who are out at the remote site right now, also make sure life support is running smoothly when they are brought in for a rest in Terra Nova. The two of them will be coming in from the remote site when Pierre LaSalle and I go out."

"I still don't understand why the remote drilling site is so important," persisted Larraine.

"You know that we're drilling for water. We are pretty confident that it's down there. We just have to work hard until we locate the water. That water is more valuable than oil on Earth. Just imagine if we had a source of liquid water on Mars. It could change our way of life and be a major step toward terraforming." Diff was enthusiastic now. "Drilling for water is probably the most important work we're doing on this planet right now."

Larraine was disappointed, but she got the point. "I guess I understand, but I really wanted to get to know you. You're famous and beautiful, and I was so excited that you would be one of my teachers."

"It sounds to me like you know how to score points with the teacher," laughed Dieffenbachia. "We will get to know each other over the time you're here, and it will be fun. For now, let's start out with asking each other one question."

"Only one?" complained Larraine.

"I have to get back to work soon," explained Diff. "I've already stretched this recess past the breaking point. So here's my question for you. That song you were singing in the green-house—what was that all about?"

The question surprised Larraine. "It was a song about the greatness of God, and how I love His awesome creation. Here I am, standing on another planet in His vast and incredible universe. The thought is almost unbelievable. I was sort of enjoying the moment—being on Mars, having interesting and challenging things to do, and meeting and working with people like you, Mrs. Maloney, and Mr. Tatsuda."

"How is it that you are so sure about God?" searched Diff.

"That's two questions," laughed Larraine. "Okay, seriously. Just look around. For instance, think about our solar system. Do you really believe it just happened?"

"Well, scientists are closing in on the Big Bang. The theory looks pretty convincing."

Larraine argued, "When have you ever seen beauty and order come out of a massive explosion? When you consider how perfect everything is for life on Earth, how can you think it just happened randomly? Each planet is traveling at just the right speed to stay in orbit along its path around the Sun."

"I sure can't argue with any of that," agreed Diff. "I just have a hard time believing in an all-powerful something that actually cares about people. After all, in my life—well, never mind. It's just that if there is such a being, He seems light years away from me."

"That's not His choice, but yours," suggested Larraine. "Want to change that?"

"I'll think about it, but not this sol." Diff was uncomfortable and decided to change the subject. "Now it's your turn to ask me a question."

"Okay." Larraine had been waiting for this. "How do you and Scott know each other?"

Diff frowned. "What makes you think we do?"

"I can tell by how Scott looks at you and you won't look at him."

"We were in astronaut training together. That's how we know each other."

"And?" Larraine raised her eyebrows, expecting to hear more.

"Sorry, Larraine, but I don't know you that well yet. The story is classified information in my personal—not personnel—file," Diff huffed.

"I guess I am prying," Larraine apologized, "but I like both of you, and it looks like you're both hurting when you're around each other for some reason. I wish I could help. On the journey, I began to think of Scott as this big, tough protective wall, but he seemed to crumble when we got here. Why is that?"

"I can't psychoanalyze his problems."

"But you know what they are," insisted Larraine.

Diff's demeanor frosted over. "His problems are his deal that he'll have to solve for himself. Now I've got to pack my gear for the morning. I'll see you later." With no further word, she sprang from her stool, whisked away her coffee cup, and steamed out of the cafeteria.

Oh great! Larraine was miserable. She put her head in her hands and sighed. *Have I made her hate me? Oh Lord, please touch her heart and show her that I truly care about her. And show me how I can help her and Scott.* Slowly raising her head, Larraine was surprised to see a tiny form dressed in a dazzling red emerging from inside the kitchen nook of the cafeteria. It was Sachiko Tatsuda. Sachiko was busy, stocking foods for the approaching dinner hour. Shyly, Larraine called out, "Hi."

Sachiko turned around in surprise, as she had not realized anyone was in the cafeteria. Smiling, she responded, "Hi yourself." Then setting her load on the counter, she gracefully glided over to the table occupied by Larraine. "You must be Larraine Temple. I've heard many good things about you from my brother."

"You're right. I'm Larraine. I've wanted to meet you."

"Well, here I am."

"I'm really curious about something," began Larraine. "How is it that both you and Mr. Tatsuda ended up on Mars?"

"First of all, I think you should forget the Mr. Tatsuda stuff. Around here, we all like to go by first names." Sachiko's brown eyes expressed friendliness inside her thickly lashed eyelids. She sat down across from Larraine. "Let's see, where shall I begin?"

Larraine sat up straight as her interest kicked into high gear. Then she noticed how she dwarfed Sachiko, and she unconsciously began to slump down in her seat. "Well, I just think it is so unbelievable that you are twins and both on Mars. And you didn't arrive at the same time, did you?"

"Hiro and I have always been very close, even when we were children," Sachiko began. "We both loved learning about space and the planets. When we entered the university and studied for our degrees, we continued to follow what was happening in space. After completing our studies, we applied to UNSEF to become astronauts. We dreamed of going to Mars. UNSEF, as you know, is a whole world organization, and it prides itself on employing people from all nations. At the time, Japan was under-represented, and we were hired right away."

"Amazing," Larraine interjected.

"What was even more amazing, is that a few months later, Terra Nova was requesting a dietician, because there were concerns about settlers getting all of the nutrients they needed, and at that time, no one with a good nutrition background had ever been stationed here. I was offered the chance, and I took it."

"So you came before Hiro?"

"Yes, and it was one of the hardest things I've ever done. I mean, I wanted to come, but as I told you, Hiro and I are very close. I knew I would miss him terribly, and I did. The truly astonishing thing is that two years later, UNSEF had great concerns about the state of plant life on Mars. The first settlers had planted many of the varieties of plants in the greenhouse, but the plants weren't really being cared for properly. For years, UNSEF just sent engineers, geologists, and pilots to Mars. Finally they realized that maybe they should send other types of scientists as well."

"So they picked Mr. Tatsuda, I mean Hiro, to come?"

"Not at first," Sachiko replied. "You may not know it, but Sandy Maloney is a world renowned botanist, and she worked for NASA. UNSEF asked her to consider going."

"Obviously, she said yes," remarked Larraine.

"She did, but with certain stipulations. She let UNSEF know that she would only stay for two years. They accepted that, because they wanted her so badly. But it wasn't good enough for Sandy. She told them she would go for two years *only* if UNSEF would send a second knowledgeable person who could take over when she left. Hiro was highly qualified, and UNSEF was happy to send another person from Japan. So two years after me, my brother arrived."

"That's an incredible story."

"I've got to get back to work, Larraine, but I've enjoyed meeting you and talking with you. Whenever you are in the cafeteria, be sure to say hello. I'm usually back in the kitchen."

"I will," replied Larraine. "I do have one more question, though."

"What's that?"

Larraine smiled as she held up her glass. "What in the world is in this juice?"

CHAPTER 12

FORGIVENESS

As the sun began to peek over the distant eastern horizon, casting a beautiful rosy glow to the surrounding highlands, a small group gathered at the rover and robot shed to say good-bye to Dieffenbachia and Pierre. Silently, each was glad not to be taking the grueling trip out to the remote drilling site.

Cheerful Chang Lee was giving them last minute instructions and warnings. "I've loaded plenty of tanks of air for the two of you. The batteries are fully charged and will keep you going until the Sun can take over in about an hour. Then you'll have a good ten hours of sunlight to run on solar energy. That should get you the 40 kilometers to Red City with time to spare. Don't stop for sight-seeing on the way, though."

"There *is* the most romantic spot about 10 kilometers out," teased Pierre.

Inside her helmet, Diff rolled her eyes. Though no one could see her eyes, they didn't need to. Her body language showed that she was not amused.

Chang could not resist. "Too bad there won't be anyone along who would enjoy it with you."

All of the Temples had arisen early to be part of the send-off group. Larraine especially wanted to tell Diff good-bye and apologize for being too forward the sol before. Pavel, Rod, Tony, and Sandy were there as well.

Sandy pulled Diff aside. She knew she could not say anything privately, as anything audible would be broadcast through everyone's headsets. She put up her hand, which held a note. The note said, *Be careful out there. I'm praying for you.*

Diff nodded her thanks.

Chang was not through giving instructions. "As soon as you get there, plug the battery in and let it recharge for at least a sol before Max and Jenny drive it back."

Pavel added, "I want it back in one piece. Watch where you're going. Don't run into any boulders or fall into any ravines."

"Are you two through?" asked Pierre. "We need to get started."

Rod stepped forward. "In two weeks, we'll send Max and Jenny back out, and Diff, you and Aaron will come back in. That will give you a little time before you take a stint on Hope. Now both of you be careful."

"Don't worry Rod. We've done this before." Diff was confident.

"Just don't get careless. When things seem routine and you let down your guard, that's when accidents happen," Rod preached.

Larraine stepped toward Dieffenbachia and said, "I hope we can get together again before you relieve Mr. Delaney on the Orbiter."

"We definitely will," answered Diff. "You can even ask me another question."

Larraine smiled to herself, recognizing that Diff was no longer upset with her. She looked forward to spending more time with the beautiful astronaut. Then as she perused the group who had come to say farewell, she realized that Scott was not part of the crowd. *What is the story with Scott and Diff?* she asked herself.

Pierre and Dieffenbachia climbed aboard the transport, waved good-bye and slowly drove to the North. Behind them swirled the millions of red fines disturbed by the wheels of the vehicle. The barely risen sun shone a point of brightness through the pinkish haze, bathing them all in a feeling of pseudo-warmth.

Later, Scott was eating lunch alone, when Larraine and Andrew approached. "Could we eat with you, Scott?" asked Andrew.

"Sure," Scott answered. "I reserved these seats just for you."

As the Temple kids sat down, Scott asked, "So after a week, how do you like Terra Nova? Are you ready to go back to Earth yet?"

"No way." Andrew was surprised that Scott could ask such a thing. "I'm learning all about the robots and rovers, including how to repair them. I'd never get a chance to do that on Earth."

"What about you, Larraine?"

"I'm not as excited about being here as Andrew is, but I'll give it a chance. What about you, Scott? Are you glad to be here?"

"Sure," affirmed Scott. "Unlike you, I had a choice about coming here. I've wanted to come here for a long time."

"Why did you want to come?" asked Larraine.

"Now that's a good question. I'm not really sure. I remember I started thinking about it way back when I was in fifth grade and we learned about the planets in the Solar System. The first trip to Mars had been successful, and it just all seemed so exciting. I started thinking that I wanted to do that. I wanted to walk on Mars some day. Maybe it's a spirit of adventure that mankind has always had. Maybe it's that I wanted to do something that very few people get the chance to do. Maybe I thought I could make a difference in life by coming. I don't know."

In no time at all, Andrew wolfed down his lunch and was raring to go. "I'm going to go back out and help Chang and Pavel with the robots. I'll see you two later."

"Wait a minute," warned Larraine. "Does Mom know you're going back out again?"

"She won't care, Rainy. I need to get back out there."

"You go tell her first. It's just like at home. We aren't supposed to go anywhere without asking first. Knowing where you are is even more important here on Mars."

"Your sister is right," Scott agreed. "The Terra Nova rule is that no one is allowed to go anywhere off base without another person along. The robot shed is close enough that you don't have to have another person, but you certainly have to let people know where you are. What if we got word of a wind storm? We need to know where everyone is."

"All right," Andrew grumbled. "I think it's dumb when I'm just going outside a few feet," but he grudgingly headed toward the Temple pod.

As they watched Andrew leave, Scott turned to Larraine. "I heard you've been working in the greenhouse."

"Yes," affirmed Larraine. "I'm learning tons about growing plants here. Working in the greenhouse is pretty interesting. I'm amazed at the variety of plants we have on Mars and how well they grow." The teenager was eager to list some of the fruits and vegetables. "Do you realize that we have corn, beans, peas, potatoes, strawberries, and fruit trees in there? There is even a dark closet where mushrooms are growing on the waste from the plants, like corn husks."

Scott nodded. "Scientists theorized that the Martian soil would be good for growing plants, and we know the atmosphere has plenty of carbon dioxide for them. The trick was keeping it warm enough, since the below freezing outdoor temperature would kill most of our plants. The greenhouse provides a great growing environment."

Larraine became thoughtful. *How do I ask him about*

Diff? She lifted her eyes to see Scott looking at her with a bemused expression. "You haven't been listening to me, have you?" he asked. "I'll give you a quarter for your thoughts."

"A quarter won't do me any good on Mars. What could I buy with it?"

"Save it for when you go home."

"Keep your quarter, Scott," smiled Larraine. *Well, here goes,* she thought. "This morning a group of us went to give Dieffenbachia and Pierre a send-off. Where were you?"

Scott shrugged. "I was sleeping."

Larraine disagreed. "I know better than that. I spent seven months on a spaceship with you and you are always the earliest riser, no matter when you go to sleep."

"You're right. I can't fool you. I just didn't feel like going out to the shed this morning. I had plenty to do in my hab."

"Scott," Larraine sighed, then summoned her courage and asked, "What's up with you and Ms. Bateman?"

"What makes you think anything is up?" Scott frowned darkly and looked away.

"It's pretty obvious, Scott. You avoid each other. You look sad every time she's around or even mentioned. Maybe I'm prying, but I really care about the two of you, and if there's any way I can help, I'd like to."

Scott's eyes were misty, as he shook his head. "You can't help, Larraine. No one can help."

"You might be right that I can't help, but God can. We could pray about it," insisted Larraine.

"No. It's all my fault. I'm just going to have to live with the fact that I blew it with Diff."

Larraine was persistent. "Well, tell me what happened. I won't tell anyone else."

"I'll tell you, but you have to promise that you won't talk about it with Dieffenbachia."

"Maybe it would help," suggested Larraine.

"No. It won't help. Do you promise?"

"All right," Larraine reluctantly agreed.

Scott began his woeful tale. "Diff and I were in astronaut training together. The first moment I saw her, so beautiful, tiny, and vulnerable, I knew that my purpose in life was to be her protector."

"Vulnerable? Ms. Bateman?"

"I know. She seems really strong, but underneath that tough exterior, she's a lonely, little girl, longing for someone to love and protect her."

"What do you mean?" Larraine could not keep the surprise out of her voice.

"Diff has been alone for some time. No family or friends to speak of. Her dad deserted her and her mom when Diff was just little, so she's never known him. Her mother died a few years ago, leaving her totally on her own. People have tried to get close to Diff, but she pushes them away. She doesn't trust anyone. She once trusted me, but as I said, I blew it."

Larraine waited for Scott to continue his story, wondering what he could have possibly done to so alienate Dieffenbachia.

"As I said, we met when we were both training to be astronauts. We became very good friends, and in fact, I wanted to be more than a friend. I'd have to say that I was in love with Diff. And I think she felt that way about me too. The two of us were at the top of the class, and NASA invited us to apply for the next Mars mission with UNSEF. Neither of us had to think twice about it. We were more than ready for the challenge, and we excitedly completed our applications and began dreaming about going to Mars together."

"Sounds romantic," said Larraine, dreamily.

"I guess it was. That is until we got our notices. Diff was selected, but I was put on hold. NASA said they decided to just send one pilot, and since Diff also had an engineering degree, she was more qualified than I. It seems silly now, but I was crushed at the time. It was like all of my training and effort were chained to an anchor and thrown into the sea. Diff tried to console me. She told me that I'd be on the next mission and meet her on Mars. That turned out to be the case, but I was mad at her at the time. I said some things I wish I'd never said. I was so crushed, I even told her I hoped I'd never see her again. With tears in her eyes, she told me, 'That can be arranged,' and she walked away from me."

Larraine was mesmerized. "You really did blow it, Scott. But I sort of understand how you were feeling."

"The thing is, Diff was not at fault, but I acted like she was. When I realized how stupid I had been, it was too late. I tried and tried to tell her I was sorry and that I didn't mean it, but she wouldn't talk to me. When I'd phone, she'd say something like, 'You don't ever want to see me—well, I don't ever want to talk to you.'"

"I understand why Ms. Bateman was upset with you, Scott." Larraine chose her words carefully. "But you really are sorry. She needs to forgive you. Have you asked her to?"

"I've tried." Scott dejectedly hung his head. "She won't talk to me or even be near me. I can't blame her. I don't deserve to be forgiven."

"That's not true," argued Larraine. "Everyone has the right and the need to be forgiven. There isn't one person on Earth (or Mars for that matter) who is perfect. Like the Bible says, *'All have sinned and fall short of the glory of God.'* "

"Now you sound like my Sunday School teacher."

Larraine became very serious. "Have you ever asked God to forgive you for your sins?"

"No. I guess I never thought I did much that was wrong. That was before I treated Diff so shamefully."

"Well the Bible is pretty clear that everyone is a sinner and that sin separates us from God. Sin keeps us from knowing God's love and plan for us. Even more, the Bible says that the result of sin is death."

"Everyone dies, Larraine."

"Physically yes, but the spirit lives on."

Scott smiled. "I'd like to believe that."

"Then listen." Larraine was adamant. "The Bible also says that *'God demonstrates His own love for us in this: while we were still sinners, Christ died for us.'* Our sin separated us from God, but God sent Jesus to die for us so we wouldn't have to be separated from Him. Jesus took our sin on Himself and paid the ultimate sacrifice by dying for us. If we believe in Jesus, the Bible says, *'If you confess with your mouth 'Jesus is Lord,' and believe in your heart that God raised him from the dead, you will be saved.'* "

"If you went to Sunday school, you must remember *John 3:16, 'For God so loved the world that He gave his one and only Son, that whoever believes in him shall not perish but have eternal life.'*"

Scott was thoughtful. "I do remember that verse, but I never really understood what it meant."

"It means that no matter what you've done, if you trust in Jesus, you are forgiven and you become a new person. You have eternal life. Ms. Batman may or may not ever forgive you, but God will if you ask, and that's more important. And when God forgives you, you can also forgive yourself."

"Is that possible?" Scott was honestly seeking. "How can I trust in Jesus?"

Larraine responded, "Do you believe God is real?"

"Yes, I'd be a fool to think the universe just happened."

"Do you believe the Bible is true?"

Scott thought a moment before he answered, "Yes, I guess so, though I never thought much about it."

"The Bible says that you have to first recognize that you are a sinner and that you need to be forgiven. Then you need to understand that Jesus died, so that you could be forgiven. Jesus said, *'I am the way and the truth and the life. No one comes to the Father except through me.'* You receive Christ by turning away from your sin and trusting Him to come into your life and forgive you. You receive Jesus by faith. You can do that right now, Scott."

The wheels were turning fast in Scott's head and heart. Even before his falling out with Diff, he had felt that something was missing in his life. He wondered if God was what he needed to fill the hole in his heart. With all his being, he wanted to believe. "I want to be forgiven, Larraine. Can you help me?"

"I can help you with a prayer, Scott. Why don't you repeat this prayer with me?" Phrase by phrase, Larraine led Scott in a prayer of faith: "I know that I need you, Lord Jesus. Thank you for giving your precious life for my sins. Thank you for forgiving my sins and giving me eternal life. Be in charge of my life now, and help me to be the person you want me to be."

When they were finished, Larraine asked, "Do you mean that prayer, Scott?"

"I do mean it."

"Then according to the Bible, you can be sure that you have been forgiven. Romans 8:38 and 39 are two of my favorite verses in the Bible. They say, *'For I am convinced that neither death nor life, neither angels nor demons, neither the present nor the future, nor any powers, neither height nor depth, nor anything else in all creation, will be able to separate us from the love of God that is in Christ Jesus our Lord.'"*

CHAPTER 13

EXPLORING THE CAVE

In the middle of their second week on Mars, Larraine and Andrew were excitedly donning their spacesuits. They were going on a field trip out to the cave with Rory Galveston this morning. Both were looking forward to getting away from Terra Nova for a few hours, and Larraine had to admit that spending the time with Rory seemed appealing.

It's not like putting on a jacket to go outside, thought Larraine. First she struggled into the temperature control garment that had many layers including tubes of flowing water to take away extra heat. It reminded her of long underwear. Next came the pressure control garment, which also resembled long underwear, but was bigger. Larraine knew that the garment would inflate somewhat to create the pressure her body needed to protect it in the Martian out-of-doors.

The bulky space boots were airproof and insulated, with special treaded soles for walking on the rocky surface of Mars. The boots connected to the lower torso assembly that was made of many layers to retain pressure, protect from a puncture, and block radiation from the sun. The bottom assembly then connected with an upper torso assembly, effectively air proofing the wearer's body.

"Rainy, you look fat and clumsy," teased Andrew.

"And you think you look better?" Larraine retorted. "Let's get our helmets, gloves, and life support systems on. Dr. Galveston won't want to wait for us, and he must already be at the rover shed, since we haven't seen him."

They finished dressing and double checked connections, paying special attention to the power display module built into the chest of each spacesuit. Larraine was having second thoughts as they stepped into the seemingly too small airlock. *I sure hope this field trip is worth the effort.* She was uncomfortably aware of the extra weight she was packing on her slender form. *Like walking around with an elephant on my shoulders,* she surmised, remembering that the suit weighed 40 kilograms on Mars.

As they exited the airlock into the frigid Martian air, an incredible sight greeted them. It was just before sunrise, and the entire sky had that usual, beautiful, rosy overtone. But there was something extra on this sol. Splattered across the pink horizon were hundreds of wispy blue-green clouds. The children had never seen anything but pink sky in their short stay on the Red Planet so far, and their eyes were drawn to the canopy above them, even though they had been warned over and over to watch their feet. Falling on the rocky terrain could be deadly if you tore a hole in your spacesuit.

Rory met them at the rover shed in good spirits. "Another beautiful Martian morning," his voice crackled into their head-sets. "Cold and dry with no possibility of rain."

"Why are there blue clouds this morning?" asked Andrew.

"There must be a lot of water ice in the atmosphere," guessed Rory. "The water ice reflects that blue color. It is quite stunning, isn't it?"

Andrew was perplexed. "If there is a lot of water ice in the atmosphere, why doesn't it ever rain?"

"Strange, isn't it?" Rory answered. "It all has to do with the atmospheric pressure. You know you have to wear the spacesuit for several reasons. You need to have oxygen flowing, because you can't get it from the Martian air, you need protection from the freezing temperatures, and you also need pressurization when you are outside. The Martian atmospheric pressure is so small, if there was water, it would boil away."

"I don't get it."

"Have you ever gone camping in the mountains, Andrew?"

"Yes."

"Water boils really quickly in the mountains, because the atmospheric pressure isn't as great as it is at sea level. Here, the atmosphere's pressure is barely there. If the water ice melted, it would immediately boil away to become vapor. That's called sublimation. So it will never rain on Mars—unless we terraform it sometime in the future."

"Weird," commented Andrew.

"Here's something else that's weird," added Rory. "Look up there." He pointed overhead.

Larraine and Andrew were surprised to see an odd shaped blot in the sky between the clouds. "What is it?" asked Larraine.

"That is Deimos, the smallest Martian moon. You don't often see either of the moons from the Martian surface, but it appears that the sky conditions are just right and the Sun's rays are reflecting perfectly this morning. Usually there are so many fines floating around that it is hard to see moons, stars, or planets. For some reason, the sky is clearer than usual this morning."

Larraine smiled. The sol was off to a great start, and she was sure they were going to have a wonderful time. Who wouldn't want to go exploring a cave with Rory Galveston? The three explorers loaded air tanks, ropes, electronic lanterns, and tools onto N3 and began the short jaunt out to the cave.

As they approached the washout area, Larraine was amazed at how gray all the rocks were. "I thought the entire terrain was red, but most of the rocks are gray. I was telling my friends back on Earth about it."

"It's a common misconception," Rory replied. "The dust-like fines cause the red color. Everyone knows the red comes from rusted iron. The tiny particles are red because of that. The bigger geological specimens are just about the same color as most Earth rocks. However, most of the big rocks have a dusting of the red fines sitting on their surfaces from former dust storms. The fines are so light, it takes very little to make them move. In fact, you can see clouds of them that our footsteps are leaving suspended. They cover everything on this planet."

"How can there be rust if it never rains?" Andrew was finding it all really confusing.

"Millions of years ago, it might have rained," replied Rory. "Besides, even without rain, remember that there is lots of water vapor in the air."

"Where is the cave?" Andrew's curious mind was on to other things.

"We're almost there. It's just behind that opening in the ridge."

Andrew tried to run ahead, but Rory immediately put a stop to that. "No running out here, Andrew. If you fell and tore a hole in your spacesuit, we would not be able to save you. We're all sticking together."

"But I have a repair patch in my spacesuit pocket," argued Andrew. "Wouldn't that repair any holes?"

"Sure, if we could find the hole. Believe me, you do not want to puncture your suit."

Andrew unhappily did as Rory demanded, but promised himself that he would somehow do some exploring on his own once they reached the cave. *He'll be too busy with his geology stuff, and Larraine will be too busy watching him. They won't notice if I wander off.*

The area was a banquet of rocks and boulders for the eyes of anyone interested in geology. They were all sizes and shapes and everywhere. The massive ridges on either side of the three explorers displayed curtain-like undulations of solid rock walls. Ahead of them spread waves of brownish-orange dust dunes. Their pathway was strewn with grey pebbles and larger rocks and boulders. Off to the left, before the distant ridge, they could see the impact basin of a long-ago meteorite.

"What kinds of rocks are these?" wondered Larraine.

"Most of them that we've tested have turned out to be like Earth's andesite, which is produced by cycles of melting and solidifying. So we suspect the rocks in this area came from volcanoes."

"Are there volcanoes near us?" Andrew was suddenly interested again.

"Not that we know of, but don't forget that the volcanoes on Mars are huge, and at one time were probably quite explosive. Sammy and I also think that there might be a volcanic crater under the polar ice cap that we can't see because of the covering of ice."

"Why are some of the rocks so smooth?" asked Larraine, picking up a specimen that she imagined was silky to the touch. "Doesn't that prove there was water here once?"

"We like to think so," responded Rory, "but not necessarily. The smooth rocks are eroded, and water sure does that. Yet so does wind, and we all know that Mars is famous for its wind storms."

The threesome had climbed through the opening in the ridge, and they could see the cave before them, like a black mouth in the wall, opening to swallow them. They scrambled over boulders, getting nearer and nearer until they stopped just before the opening. Larraine felt chills up and down her spine as she gazed at the beastly thing. *Don't be silly,* she reprimanded herself. *It's just a cave in a wall. Rory's been inside, and there's no life on Mars other than us.* Still, she couldn't shake the uncomfortable feeling that had taken hold of her.

In contrast, Rory and Andrew were enthusiastic and eager to get inside.

They had removed ropes, lanterns, and tools from N3 while Larraine had been staring at the gaping hole in the wall. Realizing that she should be helping them, Larraine picked up as much as she could carry and reluctantly followed the two guys into the cave.

Once inside, she was surprised at how expansive the cave was. The three Terra Novans were standing and even Rory had a good half meter of space above his head. The space seemed about the size of her bedroom at home, and even appeared to have a closet tucked into the opposite end from the entrance. She thought the "closet" was probably a continuation of the cave, but from where she was, it looked like a darkened indentation in the cave wall. The cave walls were very smooth—nothing like some of the limestone caves that had captivated her on Earth. She imagined a gigantic being boring a hole in the side of the cliff with a huge apple corer. Rory was in front of the wall where he had removed his specimen from his only trip to the cave. He was completely engrossed in his examination of it. Larraine was surprised by the striations of color and understood why the geologist would be enthralled by them.

"Why are the walls so smooth?" she broke the solitude.

"Good question," Rory commented. "I don't really know, but if there is a volcano under the ice cap, it could be a lava tube."

"What caused the three colors of rock in the wall here?"

"The answer to that, I can sort of tell you. After careful analysis of the sample I took, I know that the white is mostly a calcite, the black is basalt, and the red color is hematite. Previously, we haven't found much calcite on Mars, and it, along with the hematite, could be an indication that there was once a sea here. That's a pretty exciting discovery in our search for life. Why all three colors are meshed together in this wall, I don't know. I'm still trying to think of a theory for that."

Larraine was surprised that she was finding the geological aspects of the field trip interesting. However, she still didn't like being inside the cave, and continually looked toward the entrance to assure her that light was close by. The electronic lanterns were helpful, but she still did not like the closed in feeling she was experiencing.

"What do you think, Andrew? Pretty amazing, isn't it?" Larraine's question evoked no response, so she turned around to see what Andrew was doing. Her heart took off like a rocket when she realized that Andrew was not in the cave's entry room with them. "Dr. Galveston, Andrew isn't here!"

Rory was not concerned. "He's probably carrying more equipment in from N3."

Larraine hurried back outside, but N3 was all alone, its metallic sheen glistening in the rising Sun. *Where could he be?* Larraine became frantic.

Thrilled to be inside the cave, Andrew was anxious to explore. As Larraine and Rory were examining the striated wall, he headed right for the opening in the back of the cave wall. He held the lantern into the opening, and was pleased to see that it was a tunnel. The tunnel was not as roomy as the entry of the cave, but it was easily passable. In fact, as he entered it, he was delighted to find that he could walk in it comfortably by just bending slightly. The tunnel curved to the right after about 10 meters; then it progressed slightly uphill. The heavy spacesuit and the incline combined to slow Andrew down and push his breathing rate up.

Approaching the top of the incline, Andrew could see that the tunnel opened into a larger room. He cautiously held the lantern out in front of him and gasped. The room was a pit, deep and dark, surrounded by a small ledge. Andrew knelt down and held the lantern out, but could not discern the bottom of the pit. What he could see, skyrocketed his curiosity off the charts. The pit's walls were reflective and even sparkling in places. It gave the illusion of being mirrored and studded with diamonds. *I need to tell Rory and Larraine about my geological discovery.* Andrew couldn't wait to share his find.

The eleven-year-old quickly rose to his feet and turned to retrace his steps. In his haste, he dropped the lantern and it went clattering noisily down the abyss. In the pitch black, he felt for the sides of the tunnel, but he could not find them. He knew they were close; he had barely moved away from them. "Larraine! Rory!" Andrew screamed. "I'm lost in the dark! Oh, help me God!"

In the cave entrance, Larraine gasped as she heard her brother's cry for help. She and Rory immediately grabbed their lanterns and headed for the tunnel, since it was the only opening in the cave. "Be calm," Rory instructed. "You never hurry in a cave, because you don't know what you're going to run into. He'll be all right if he just stands still. Stay where you are, Andrew. We're coming for you."

In frightened frustration, Andrew backed up to turn to the left and search for the tunnel in that direction, when his feet began to slip. Sliding backward, his hands frantically grasped for anything to stop his slide, but they came up with nothing but the thin Martian air. His backward slip picked up momentum, and he began to career down the side of the abyss. He went faster and faster, and there was nothing he could latch onto to slow his descent. The wall was like glass, and more slick than a mid-winter ski hill. Just as it seemed his drop would never end, his feet hit solid ground with a thud that jarred his entire body. Andrew's nearly disastrous plunge had been averted by a ledge that stuck out just a little more than a meter from the wall of the cave. The boy felt around and could tell that the edge of his saving ledge dropped off. "Help me Larraine and Rory," he wailed.

He heard Rory's firm voice, "Stay where you are, Andrew. We're on our way." Andrew could hear his sister and the geologist breathing heavily as they climbed the incline to the pit. He heard Rory take a deep breath and then swear, "Martian Meteorites! Where are you, Andrew?"

Andrew could see the light from the lantern above him. He had slid about 10 meters into the pit. All the way to the top, the walls looked as slick as glass. The only imperfection he could see was the ledge that had saved him from falling even farther. His voice sounded small as he said, "I'm down in the pit on a ledge." Looking up, he could see Rory's silhouette against the black backdrop of the cave wall.

"How will we get him?" Larraine cried.

"Stay here," demanded Rory. "I'll go back and get rope. We brought some and left it at the entrance to the cave."

As Rory hurried back down the tunnel's ramp, Larraine sat by her lantern and prayed. *Oh Lord, give us wisdom and help us rescue my brother.* Aloud she said, "Andrew, we're going to get you out of there. Dr. Galveston went to get some rope. Whatever you do, don't move away from that ledge you're on."

"Rainy, I'm more afraid than I was during the meteoroid storm."

"We won't leave you Andrew. God will get you out of this pit."

Larraine heard Rory's angry voice punctuated by labored breathing responding to her assertion. "It's more like Rory Galveston will get you out of this pit."

Even though only minutes had passed, it seemed like an eternity to Larraine and Andrew before Rory returned, the rope slung over his shoulder. He wearily placed his lantern on the ledge, and unwound the rope. The rope was a good 25 meters long, which he estimated would be adequate for the job. He carefully formed one end into a circle for Andrew to slip into, tying it into a square knot, and then tied the other end around his middle. Fortunately, the boy was a lot smaller than he, but he still knew pulling him up would require a great deal of effort. "Larraine, go bring extra air tanks from N3. Our exertions are going to use the air in these tanks up more quickly than usual."

"But I can't leave my brother and you," protested Larraine.

"Look Larraine, none of us will make it if we run out of air. Get the air tanks."

Larraine knew he was right, though she couldn't bear the thought of leaving them. She gritted her teeth, picked up her lantern, and started down the tunnel. The blackness just outside the light of her lantern seemed to mock her as her mind conjured numerous disturbing thoughts. *What if I lose my way? Were there any branches off this tunnel? What if I can't get the air tanks in time? What if I fall and lose my lantern?* She was beginning to cry, and that made her angry with herself. Her heart was pounding as she finally broke out into the roomy cavern entrance. Near the opening, she left the lantern and quickly climbed down to N3.

Rory's voice was loud and clear through Larraine's head set. "I'm tossing the rope down to you, Andrew. Wait for it to get to the ledge. Don't reach out for it."

Help Dr. Galveston rescue Andrew, Larraine prayed silently, as she picked up two of the air tanks. There was no way she would be able to carry three at once, so she would just have to come back for a third one after she delivered the first two.

While Larraine struggled back to the cave, she heard Andrew's excited voice. "I have the rope Rory!"

"Great," responded Rory. "Now slip the loop over your head and put both arms through it. Then I'll pull you up."

"What if the knot comes undone?"

"It won't," insisted Rory. "It's a square knot. I promise it won't come undone."

Larraine entered the cave and attached the lantern to her utility belt so she could still carry the air tanks. She smiled and was grateful that Rory's voice sounded so calm and positive. *But is he telling the truth?* Her mind was reeling.

"I'm ready," Andrew's small voice came through. "The walls are really slippery, Rory. There's nothing to hold onto."

"Just hang onto the rope. I'll have to pull you up. Here we go."

Larraine could hear that Rory was gulping for air as he began to lift Andrew. Even weighing 1/3 as much as he did on Earth, the added weight of the spacesuit was enormous, and pulling the boy straight up was extremely strenuous work. Andrew was dead weight, and there was no way for him to help.

Larraine rounded the curve of the cave and looked up the incline. Rory was backing down it with the rope tied around his waste. He was using his weight to counterbalance Andrew's, rather than just pulling with his arms.

"I'm moving up!" shouted Andrew with true relief.

"How much farther do we have to go?" groaned Rory.

"I'm over half way," yelled Andrew.

Larraine backed up. "I'm leaving the air tanks right next to the tunnel in the entry and going back for another one," she said.

"That's good, Larraine," praised Rory.

Larraine scurried back down to N3. She methodically picked up a third air tank, and looked at the sky. It looked like the sun had barely moved at all since they entered the cave. Yet it felt like they had been here for hours.

"I'm almost at the top," Andrew shouted.

"Let me know when you're there," said Rory.

Larraine made it back to the cave's roomy entrance. She set the air tank down and looked up the tunnel. Rory had not made it around the bend yet, but he must be close. She realized that he was backing up in the dark, because he had left his lantern on the ledge of the pit for Andrew. Larraine picked up her lantern and walked up around the bend where she could see Rory. She held the lantern out so he could see. "Thanks," he said.

"I'm out!" Andrew was exultant.

"Don't move." Rory's voice was rock solid. "I'm coming back to get you." He took the lantern from Larraine, and made his way laboriously back up the incline of the cave. As he moved away, the tunnel got darker and darker until Larraine could not see her glove in front of her face plate. She leaned against the tunnel, closed her eyes, and prayed, letting God's spirit comfort her fears. *I'll just wait here until they come back with the lantern,* she promised herself.

She didn't have long to wait. Soon she was aware that the tunnel was brightening, and she could see Andrew walking toward her with Rory close behind. All three wearily stumbled back to the big room, where they sat to rest and replenish their supply of air.

"Thank you for coming to get me, Rory," said Andrew, after they were all feeling safe and rested again.

"You're welcome, Andrew. But I can't excuse what you did. You've been warned and warned about going off on your own. What in Mars were you thinking?" Clearly, Rory was not happy.

"I'm sorry." Andrew knew he was in trouble. "I just wanted to go exploring on my own."

"You can't do that on Mars. I hope you've learned a lesson."

Larraine was glad that Rory was reprimanding Andrew, because she was so relieved to have him safe and sound that she didn't think she would be capable of doing it. She was expecting Rory's next words, but still found them to be a disappointment.

"Okay, we need to pack up and return to Terra Nova. We need to be sure that Andrew is okay, so this field trip is over."

CHAPTER 14

RED CITY

Scott ambled into the Communications Center for his meeting with Rod. He had been waiting impatiently to talk to the commander from the first moment The Seeker crew had arrived at Terra Nova. Still not assigned any actual duties, he was feeling pretty useless, like a pilot without an airplane. The more he thought about it, he realized that was the case. There was nothing for him to fly on the surface of Mars. He could run the shuttle between Hope and Terra Nova, but it wasn't exactly a daily, or even weekly event. He wanted to be doing something that mattered, and he hoped Rod was going to assign him to something.

As he entered the area, he knew that something unusual was going on. Tony was talking with someone through the com-link, and both Damaris and Preston Temple were hovering. Rod was stalking back and forth.

"You're sure he's okay?" Tony was asking someone. "All right. I've got his parents right here. His mom will want to check him out as soon as you get back. Do you need any help?"

Scott could see that Damaris was very agitated. She was nervously alternating between pacing back and forth and bowing her head as if she was praying.

Tony put down the com-link and turned around. "Everything is going to be okay. Try not to worry. Rory says that Andrew is fine. They're on their way back to Terra Nova, and I estimate they'll be here within the next 30 minutes."

"What happened?" Scott was concerned.

"I made a mistake," said Rod angrily. "I thought it would be a good idea for Rory to take Larraine and Andrew out to his cave for the sol. He's been begging to get out there since Sammy's been laid up, and I can't let him go alone. I thought taking the kids out would kill two birds with one stone. It would give him the chance to get out there for more rock samples, and it would be a great learning experience for the Temple kids. However, they had an accident."

"What do you mean, they had an accident?" Scott's concern was evident.

"All we know is Andrew fell into a pit," replied Tony, "but everything is okay. They got him out and he's not hurt. Scared a little, but not hurt."

"How did it happen?" Scott wanted to know.

Damaris spoke up. "We don't know the whole story for sure, but it sounds like Andrew took off on his own. That doesn't surprise me, and he's going to be in big trouble once I'm sure that he isn't hurt."

"It's Galveston's fault," steamed Rod. "I shouldn't have trusted him with your kids."

"I'm not blaming Rory," said Pres. "Andrew is too curious for his own good. We've been letting him explore here more than we ought to. We know what he's like. It's time to rein him in a little. He won't like it, but he's just shown us we can't trust him to be careful yet."

"I'm going to put on a suit and go out to meet them," said Damaris.

"I'll go with," agreed Pres.

As they left, Rod shook his head. "This was for real. That kid could have died."

Scott could tell that Rod was in a distressed mood, but he hoped the Commander would give him a job on this very sol. Uncomfortable with the situation, he began, "Uh, Rod. You wanted to see me?"

"Yeah, Scott, I did. I've been thinking about a special mission for you."

Scott perked up. "That sounds good to me."

"Max and Jenny have just come in for some R and R from Red City, and Pierre and Diff just went out there. In about a week and a half, I have to bring Diff back here so she can get ready to take over on Hope. I really would like to get Aaron in here for some rest before I have to call Diff back. So I was thinking about having you go out to Red City and relieve Aaron for awhile."

Scott was perplexed as he considered what Diff might think about the whole idea. He knew she would be very upset with his presence at the remote site. There would be no way to avoid each other there. He immediately made an excuse. "I don't know anything about drilling for water, and I don't know the way to Red City. I want to have some way to help the settlement, but I don't think going out there is the answer."

"Diff and Pierre can teach you everything you need to know. I've seen your records, and I know you can do just about anything you put your mind to. In fact, that's one of the reasons I selected you to pilot The Seeker crew. I need versatile, creative people like you in Terra Nova. Obviously, you'll be switching duties on Hope once Brian or Diff leave to pilot The Seeker back to Earth, but until then, I want to use you at Red City and for various responsibilities around here."

"But even if I could learn the drilling, how will I find my way out there?"

"Well, you won't be going alone. No one is allowed outside of Terra Nova alone. I'll be sending Chang Lee out with you. He knows the way, and he can bring Aaron in. Then in a week and a half, I'll send Jenny and Max back out, and you and Diff can return, so she can have a little time to prepare for her stint on Hope. Eventually, Pres Temple will also spend time at

Red City, but right now it's more important for him to gain an understanding of the life support system."

Inwardly, Scott groaned. He could just imagine what Diff would say about traveling all the way back into Terra Nova with just him. Rod's plan was going from bad to worse. "It's just not possible, Rod."

"What do you mean? You can do this," insisted Rod.

Scott decided he had no recourse but to tell the truth. "Um, it's a long story."

"Well make it short, because I don't have all sol." Rod was obviously displeased with Scott's attitude.

"Diff hates me, Rod. She will be madder than a stirred up hornet if you do this. You can't ask her to put up with me in a place where she can't avoid me."

Rod couldn't believe what he was hearing. "That's ridiculous," he snorted. "Diff will do whatever I say. She understands the chain of command, unlike some people around here. Chang and Pavel are already making sure the terra-rover is ready, and I'm expecting you to be on it before sunrise tomorrow."

With that, Rod walked away, leaving Scott frustrated and bewildered. *I don't understand this, Lord, but you are in control of my life now. Please soften Diff's heart and help her to forgive me.*

Scott had only been on Mars for two weeks, and already he was wondering if coming was a good idea. He could not believe how cheerful Chang was. They were finally at Red City, after eight grueling hours of crawling along in the terra-rover. The slow speed and continual bouncing had taken its toll on the huge astronaut, and he was not feeling cheerful in the least. He was so glad to view the dual connected habs against the icy polar vista, he even forgot to be worried about what Dieffenbachia Bateman would do and say.

A thick layer of what looked like snow covered the ground completely, but Scott knew it wasn't like the snow back on Earth. Much of this frosty landscape was frozen carbon dioxide rather than water ice. The scene presented a rugged beauty, with its massive tinted blue hills painted against the pinkened Martian sky. The sun was nearly setting, so its rays struck the ice, giving it a beautiful but eerie glow. *Incredible,* thought Scott. *Nothing like this exists on Earth. Even if I hadn't traveled for months through space, I would know I was on an alien world. What rare and unusual splendor.* As Scott's gaze continued to sweep the panorama before him, he noticed a third structure that he assumed must be producing the needed oxygen and water for this site, and a small flying craft. *Why are we putting up with jostling for eight hours, when we have an aircraft here?* His thoughts were interrupted as he saw two spacesuited figures leave one of the habs and wave in greeting.

"Hey Chang, what did you bring us?" Scott heard a voice he did not recognize.

"I brought your replacement, Aaron," answered Chang. "You're going back to Terra Nova with me tomorrow."

"I already knew that," said Aaron Abrahamson, the Israeli engineer, "but didn't you bring us any fresh vegetables or fruit from the greenhouse? These freeze dried dinners are getting to us out here."

"Actually, I did bring you some beans, corn, and sweet potatoes. Sachiko thought you all would like them, so she twisted my arm." Turning to look inside the terra-rover, Chang teased, "Oops. It looks like they must have fallen out on one of our major bumps along the way."

Is this guy always happy? wondered Scott. *We've just completed the most miserable eight hours of my life, and he's still having a good time.*

Chang climbed off the transport and unloaded a case of fresh food. "Hey Pierre, help me carry some of this stuff."

Every muscle in Scott's body screamed in pain as he moved to get off the vehicle. "Will my teeth ever stop knocking together again?" he asked Chang.

Chang, Aaron, and Pierre all laughed. "The first time is the hardest," said Aaron.

"No it isn't," argued Pierre. "Every time is the hardest, but welcome to Red City."

"Why Red City?" Scott wanted to know. "It's not a city, and the ice covers any red that's under it."

"We really aren't sure who came up with the name originally," explained Chang. "It was probably a joke, but if we ever do find water under the surface, you can bet a city will grow here. Since we're on Mars, I think someone decided something should have the name Red in it. Anyway, it's been called Red City for about the past eight years. People got tired of calling it the remote site. Red City sounds a lot more fun."

"Let's show you to your quarters, Scott," offered Pierre. "You're going to be bunking in the eastern pod with me. The women stay in the western one."

"Speaking of women," interrupted Chang, "Where is Diff? Why isn't she here to meet us?"

"I don't know," replied Aaron. "When we got Rod's message, she seemed really upset, and she just took off. We're sort of worried about her. She shouldn't be out by herself, and she knows it. Taking off like that isn't like her."

"You let her go?" Chang's voice was incredulous.

"Have you ever tried to stop Diff from doing something once her mind is made up?" Aaron defended himself. "Don't let her size fool you. She's unstoppable."

Chang sighed, "You're right. I wonder what got into her?"

The four men entered the Eastern hab, one at a time. It had a miniscule airlock capable of holding barely one of them at a time. Each man removed his space suit after leaving the chamber. When Scott finally entered, he was not surprised to see that it closely resembled the interior of the pods at Terra Nova. There were bunks for six people, three above and three below them. Unlike Terra Novan modules, however, this one had no upper level. Furniture was less than sparse. Scott could only see one desk and chair. A small microwave oven sat on the desktop, taking up half of its surface area. *Primitive* is what he thought.

"Where do we store our spacesuits?" was Scott's first question. There was clearly no room for closet space among the bunks.

Aaron opened a door that led to the heavy vinyl tubing connecting their pod to the western module. Immediately through the doorway was a pegged structure for hanging the spacesuits. The four men gladly put the suits away.

"You'll really learn what roughing it is like out here, Scott," began Pierre. "We have no kitchen or communal area, and only a small bathroom wedged in the tube between the habs. The only way to stretch out is to put on a spacesuit and go outside."

"I can sure see why you all need to come in for rest and relaxation once in awhile," Scott declared. "This isn't exactly a party."

"The party is the job we're doing," Aaron was quick to point out. "We really think from the readings our probes have done that liquid water is under us. We just have to find the right spot, and we'll hit it."

"Well, I'll be glad to help with the project, but as I told Rod, I don't know anything about drilling."

"Pierre and Diff can handle the technical side of things and teach you everything you need to know," Aaron told him. "You'll learn fast, and your muscle will really come in handy when we close up a drilling spot and start another."

"I noticed the flying craft outside. Why do we have to make that miserable, jerky, eight-hour trip, when there is an obvious way to get here quickly and smoothly?" Scott wanted to know.

"That craft is only for our transportation in case of emergency," Pierre informed him. "It's fueled and ready to go at all times, but we wouldn't use it just for transportation on just any sol. Did you notice the huge fold-up wings and the fact that it is made of very light materials?"

"I didn't get that close to it."

"Well, with the low atmospheric pressure here, we need a super light craft with great surface area and a lot of thrust," began Pierre's explanation. "We have limited fuel on Mars. Even though we can manufacture fuel, most of it is used for the shuttle trips between Hope and Terra Nova and to build up the supply for trips back to Earth. We've got it for an emergency situation, but otherwise, we want to conserve our fuel."

"I guess that makes sense, but I'm not looking forward to the next trip in that transport vehicle."

Chang perked up. "Well Scott, we can solve that problem for you. You can just stay out here permanently."

Everyone laughed as Scott said, "No thanks."

Dieffenbachia Bateman had been hiking around just out of sight of the Red City structures. She knew better than to be off completely on her own, but she also had no desire to be in the "city" when Chang and Scott arrived. *How could Rod do this to me? How can I manage to be in the same place with Scott Jamison for the next week and a half? If there really is a God, it's obvious He doesn't care about my feelings.* Diff's green eyes filled with tears as she remembered how much she had once cared for Scott and how he had carelessly broken her trusting heart. *Cut it out, Diff. If you start crying, you'll fog up the face plate, and then what will you do?*

Diff estimated she had about one hour of air left, and then she would need to return to the Western hab, Scott Jamison or not. She had no idea how she could work with the man or even talk to him during the time she had left out here.

Diff approached her favorite spot in the Red City vicinity. It was just behind the hill the habs sat against. All of the human structures, including the drilling spots, were hidden from view in this place. From here, no evidence of human life on the planet was visible. Massive, rugged hills covered with thick ice filled the vista as far as one could see. It was approaching dusk, and sometimes she thrilled to the view of Phobos or Deimos passing overhead. She still was awed by the pink sky and the translucent glow off the surrounding mountains. *The only thing missing from this wonderland is water,* she reminded herself. *I have to do my part to help find the water that I'm sure must be under this place.*

Diff liked to think of this hidden spot as her own personal thinking place. She came here frequently, unbeknownst to the others who inhabited Red City. She was usually only gone for 30 minutes or so. This time she'd been gone several hours, and she knew they had missed her. They were probably even worried about her. Her conscience was beginning to trouble her a little, but she still had no desire to go back and face Scott. *God, if you're there, I wish I could believe in you. I wish I knew that you were watching over me and taking care of me. I don't think you've shown me any proof of that so far in my life. So far it seems like I'm the only one who takes care of me. I'm not even sure that I like me. How can I believe that you love me?*

As usual, Diff did not hear any answer to her attempt at a prayer. She sighed, took one more longing look across the bleak and beautiful picture stretching before her, and began dragging her feet back to Red City.

CHAPTER 15

ROBOTICS

Andrew was lucky to get to continue his work with the rovers and robots, and he knew it. He had probably been in the most serious trouble of his entire 11 years when he, Larraine, and Rory had returned from the cave. There was no doubt his mom and dad loved him, but he hated their imposed consequences for his stupid stunt.

That's how he thought of it—a stupid stunt. *Why can't I be less curious? Why can't I think before I act?* he wondered. He was lucky to be alive, although his sister would have said that luck had nothing to do with it. *She's probably right,* he grudgingly admitted.

Once his parents were satisfied that Andrew was safe, they gave him the longest lecture ever in the history of parents. He was told he would be allowed to work with the bots, but he was not to go to the shed by himself. He could only go if someone was willing to walk him there. Then he was to remain in the shed with Chang or Pavel until one of them returned to the habs or until someone else had time to walk him back. In addition, his father told him he was to memorize scripture and write an essay on what he thought the scripture meant and why it applied to his situation. It was a whole list of verses from Proverbs.

Andrew hated his punishment, even as he admitted to

himself that he probably deserved it. He was trying as hard as he could to follow all of the rules, memorize his verses, and make his parents trust him again. "Five verses," Andrew complained to the robot beside him. "Don't you think three would have been enough? And an essay. That will take me forever, when I could be spending my time working on you." The boy reached in the utility pocket of his pressurized suit, withdrew and unfolded a piece of paper, and shoved it in front of the robot's camera face. "How would you like to memorize these?

> *Proverbs 4:1 Listen, my sons, to a father's instruction; pay attention and gain understanding.*
> *Proverbs 10:1 A wise son brings joy to his father, but a foolish son grief to his mother.*
> *Proverbs 14:16 A wise man fears the Lord and shuns evil, but a fool is hotheaded and reckless.*
> *Proverbs 15:5 A fool spurns his father's discipline, but whoever heeds correction shows prudence.*
> *Proverbs 15:32 He who ignores discipline despises himself, but whoever heeds correction gains understanding."*

Andrew was glad that Chang had returned from Red City with Aaron. He liked Pavel Stanislof, and the man certainly knew his stuff, but Pavel was very serious and not much fun. Chang, however, was the king of fun. His big smile and easy-going attitude made everyone feel all right.

Pavel and Chang were continually at work repairing machinery. The rovers, robots, transport vehicles, and life support systems kept them perpetually busy. After every trip to and from the Red City, they would practically take apart the terra-rover, check for any problems, tighten everything, lube it, and reassemble it. This time, they let Andrew help every step of the way. He wasn't old enough to be responsible for doing it by himself, but as he learned, he would eventually be fixing things on his own. He was confident of that. Andrew knew he learned quickly and he had a strong mechanical aptitude. Plus, he loved the bots as if they were people. He had nicknames for all of them. Better nicknames than N3, which the boy had renamed Ned.

Ned was Andrew's special project. Every time a rover was taken out in the Martian terrain, it came back covered with the red fines prevalent everywhere. Then it was necessary to carefully clean the rover, sometimes removing its toothed steel wheels and lubing them. Ned was just a basic cart with automated wheels, but Andrew could not help thinking of him in a personal way, every time he looked at his camera face.

"Thanks for transporting all those air tanks for us, Ned," Andrew told him as he polished him up. "We would have been in big trouble without them. It sure was nice of you to carry all that heavy stuff for us."

Chang and Pavel smiled as they listened to the one-sided conversation. Andrew shared their love of mechanics, so they were glad to have his company at the shed. He was also a definite asset when it came to keeping the robotic equipment serviced. The two men also expected that Andrew's help would be invaluable to Pavel while Chang was serving time on Hope.

"Hey Andrew," called Pavel from the terra-rover that he and Chang were cleaning. "We're about ready to put this wagon back together. Give us a hand."

"Sure," replied Andrew. "I was just finishing up with Ned here. I'll be right there." Turning to the bot, Andrew patted it and whispered, "See you later friend."

The boy watched carefully as the two men painstakingly put the transport back together again, assisting whenever they let him. It was a major job that had taken the two men most of the sol. The work was critical, because a breakdown somewhere between Terra Nova and Red City would be disastrous. People could walk as fast as Behemoth (Andrew's new name for the vehicle) could travel, but with spacesuits, air tanks, and the difficult terrain, it was impossible to go as far on foot.

The work in the shed was much more difficult than the same work on Earth, because the shed was not pressurized, so the mechanics had to wear their spacesuits. It took a great deal of patience and practice to repair and service the robotic equipment effectively, and the technicians took frequent breaks, returning to the living habs about every three hours. So a job like Behemoth was an all sol affair. That suited Andrew just fine, because he loved it.

After all four wheels were back on Behemoth, Andrew was disappointed to hear Chang say, "That's it for this sol, Andrew. Pavel and I need a break, and we have to take you back for your studies. We were warned to have you back by early afternoon, so you could finish your essay and your math this afternoon."

Andrew knew better than to argue. Right now he was practicing compliance. "Will I be able to come back tomorrow?" he begged.

Chang smiled. "They wouldn't dare take you away from us. We've let them know that we need your services. We'll see you tomorrow."

As the three carefully put away all of their tools and headed for the habs, Andrew's spirits were high. At least in the rover shed he was being the kind of son who would make his father proud. Now if he could just be like that with the rest of his life.

CHAPTER 16

DUST!

"Hope to Terra Nova. This is an emergency message. I repeat. This is an emergency message."

Tony's attention was immediately riveted to Brian Delaney's voice. It was the beginning of his third week on Mars, and this was the first emergency message. The wiry Canadian scrambled to push the two-way receiver button on the console, but spoke calmly into the com-link. "Terra Nova to Hope. I'm reading you loud and clear, Brian."

Brian continued, "We can see a dust storm in your area, and it is heading your way. It looks like some pretty serious wind is blowing down there, and it's whipping up a lot of dust. The storm may pass you by to the southeast, but I think you should prepare for the worst. I'm estimating that you have about 17 minutes before it reaches the settlement."

"Roger," answered Tony. "I'll let Rod know right away."

Tony immediately radioed Rod, who was out in the greenhouse. Rod instructed him to call every inhabitant of Terra Nova back to base. Fortunately, no one was farther away than the shed, so in very little time, all was secure. Rod stayed outside, making sure everyone was in, before he entered the airlock.

The commander took one last look around and could see

massive, dark red clouds building on the horizon to the south-west. The storm was definitely heading their way. He breathed a sigh of relief, knowing that everyone was inside. Whether the storm lasted three minutes, three sols, or three months, they should be safe inside the pods.

Once inside, Rod hustled to the Communication Center. "Good job, Tony. Everyone is inside. How about Red City?"

Tony's heart sank. "Red City," he whispered. "I was so busy contacting everyone here, I totally forgot about them."

"Call them right now," ordered Rod, his voice worried.

"Red City, this is Terra Nova," began Tony. He waited shortly for a response and then tried again. "Red City, this is Terra Nova. I have an emergency message. Come in, please."

Tony and Rod stood by, anxiously hoping to hear from the three explorers at Red City, but only a creepy silence answered their call.

While Terra Nova prepared for the storm, the Red City inhabitants blithely manned their drilling rig. A heavy frost hung in the air, and sparse particles of ice dropped to the ground, adding to the mounds of frozen residue already on the surface. Inside their spacesuits, the three explorers were cozy and warm and unaffected by the harsh environment from which they were protected by mere centimeters.

Diff, Pierre, and Scott fell back as the drill plunged through solid rock into a flexible substance, and steam gushed from the hole, splattering their spacesuits with blobs of orangey-brown residue. Whatever they hit came shooting out of the hole like a geyser, turning to steam before their very eyes.

Pierre was the first to give voice to what all three were thinking. "Do you think we've hit water?" He cautiously attempted to mask his exuberance.

"I'd say it's a good bet," answered Diff, excitedly.

Scott, as usual, did not feel free to say anything when he was near Diff, but he was just as enthused as the other two.

"Let's send down a vacuum capsule to collect what's under there, and keep it from sublimating," suggested Diff. "Then we can analyze what we've got and send word back to Terra Nova."

Pierre walked to the equipment rover and began to search for the vacuum capsule when he noticed that the rusted fines around his feet had begun to swirl menacingly. Footsteps always caused the dust to lift in mini-clouds around the settlers' feet, but this was different. He was standing still, and the tiny particles were airborne as high as he could see. His heart leaped in his chest, and he looked toward Diff and Scott to see if they had noticed anything. Both were mesmerized by the geyser and oblivious to the impending disaster.

Pierre tried not to panic. He grabbed a vacuum capsule, walked back to the other two, and calmly said, "I think we have a dust storm coming. We'd better take our sample and get to safety."

Diff could not believe what she was hearing. She looked around. To the southwest, she could see boiling red clouds of dust towering miles into the sky. Martian dust storms were legendary; commencing in the southern hemisphere during its summer season, the storms could rapidly encircle the entire planet, easily covering thousands of kilometers. They could come up suddenly and last for months at a time. She had never seen one before, and she certainly didn't want to be in one now. Thoughts of the nightmare raged inside her mind.

"Leave the equipment, and let's go," she shouted. "There's no time to take a sample." Diff didn't wait to see if the men were following, but immediately turned and headed for shelter, attempting to outrun the storm and her dream. She was breathing rapidly as her unreasonable fear took control.

Although they wanted a sample of their discovery, the men followed, knowing it would be dangerous to stay where they were. They were a good ten minutes away from protection, so there was no time to waste.

Scott was not really afraid, as he had read extensively about the Martian dust storms. He knew the winds blew fiercely–easily 150 kilometers an hour or more–but with the low atmospheric pressure, it wouldn't be like a windstorm of that magnitude on Earth. He understood from his reading that the wind itself would not do much damage; it would only cause a massive dust storm. Scott was more concerned about losing visibility than being hurt by the wind itself. So far there was plenty of visibility, but he didn't want to chance losing it.

The pathway to Red City was still clear, and it had been traveled so often over the past few years that it was well worn. The going was easy, but the habs were still beyond a hill and not yet visible. The three hurried along, plagued by the increasing particles of dust surrounding them. They could tell the wind had picked up, and the fines were being blown more fiercely. The particles knocked against their helmets, audibly reminding them of their need to get inside.

Terrified, Diff could not get her dream out of her mind. She scrambled as fast as she could, intent upon getting back to the safety of the habs. She felt strangely as if she had lived this before and didn't like the conclusion of the story. She could still see a good 30 meters ahead of her, but her fear convinced her that the dust was thickening with every step.

Soon the full force of the storm was upon them, blowing as mightily as it could in the thin Martian air. They could feel it pushing them around somewhat, but were in no danger of being blown over. The explorers were looking through a hazy, thin red fog, as visibility continued to decrease.

Dieffenbachia Bateman panicked. The storm worsened. The dust swirled, darkening the sky with an eerie brown-orange tint. The fines crackled as they blew against her helmet, pelting as if trying to penetrate it. The wind, the fines, the crackling—Diff finally lost control and tried to run in her cumbersome spacesuit.

"Diff, stop running!" shouted Scott, fearfully.

Diff paid no attention to Scott. Terror took complete control of her senses. Looking into the distance, searching for the sight of the habs, she failed to see the small boulder that caught her foot, and she fell forward brutally. She put out her hands to break her fall, but her knee made direct contact with a sharp rock, the impact causing excruciating pain and puncturing her suit. She writhed on the ground, trying but unable to stand, helplessly feeling the pressurization protecting her body diminishing. "Please God, help me!" she screamed. "Pierre! Scott! Help me!"

Scott couldn't believe his eyes when Diff fell. "Diff!" he yelled.

"Help me," Diff whimpered. "I've torn a hole in my suit and I can't walk. I can feel the pressure leaking out." She frantically and clumsily tried to undo the pocket that contained patching for her suit.

"Pierre, help us," Scott called. But the contagion of panic controlled Pierre, and he raced for the habs, ignoring his two colleagues. "Pierre, Diff needs help. Help us." Ignoring Scott's pleas, Pierre headed for safety.

Help me save her, Lord, prayed Scott as he rushed to Diff's side. "Diff, I won't leave you. I'll get you back to the habs."

"I'm not going to make it," gasped Diff. Her breathless voice was soft as she resigned herself to the impending unconsciousness. "Give me another chance, God. Please save me. I'll give my life to you. Please." She struggled to get the words out. "Save—yourself—Scott.   You—never—wanted—to—see—me—a—gain."

"Diff, I care about you more than anything. I'm not leaving you. I'll get your suit patched and take you back. Keep talking to me."

But Scott heard only silence. Diff was unconscious.

Scott anxiously removed the patch kit from his utility pocket. It wasn't easy to peel the backing with his gloves on, but he determined to do it. He raced against time, knowing Diff had less air and pressurization every second. Without air, she could only live a few minutes. Without pressurization, her blood would boil. He had to patch the hole in seconds, or there was no hope. "Help me, Lord," he breathed aloud.

Finally managing to grasp the pull tab, Scott jerked the backing off the patch. *Now if I can just find the hole.* Bending over Diff's leg, he looked for an obvious tear, but couldn't see one. He could, however, tell where the rock had hit her knee, because the suit fabric was smudged. The patch was large enough to cover the entire soiled area, so Scott breathed another prayer and applied the patch. Wanting to be absolutely sure that no air or pressure could now escape, Scott also pulled a clamping tool out of his pocket. He clamped over the likely holed area. Then he bent over and struggled to lift the stricken woman. Diff was tiny, but the suit she wore weighed more than 40 kilograms on Mars. Could he possibly carry her the remaining distance to safety? Pulling her into a sitting position, Scott slung Diff over his shoulder. She was limp and motionless, and he prayed she was still alive. With intense determination, Scott slowly stood, using all of his power and strength to lift Diff. *Help me Lord,* he prayed again.

The dusty air had continued to thicken, but there was still some visibility. Scott knew his way, and he carefully stuck to the worn path. He could not see the habs yet, but knew they were close; he estimated not more than 5 minutes away. He was reasonably sure that the hole was sealed, so his biggest concern was how much air was left in Diff's air tank. Even if he made it to the pods in 5 minutes, it wouldn't be fast enough if she was out of air.

Scott picked up the pace, breathing heavily of his own supply of air, with the extra exertion of carrying Diff. Her spacesuit weight plus the weight of his own spacesuit gave him a staggering load. Scott was tempted to run, but knew that even if it was possible, running might prove yet more disastrous to both of them. He willed himself to walk steadily, but as quickly as he could. Even though the air was saturated with the pelting dust, he could still see the pathway, and he knew that it led right to Red City. Scott paid attention to the ground and trusted that the path would take him and his precious load to sanctuary.

It was as dark as night now, with the dusty air shrouding the sunlight, but Scott was amazed to notice that he could still see where he was going. Perhaps everything he had read about the Martian storms was true, and there would still be visibility through the myriad of suspended particles. As far as he knew, no one had ever been caught out in a storm before, so no one knew how bad the visibility would be from inside one. He began to feel cautiously optimistic that he and Diff would make it.

As his confidence grew, Scott saw a darker area ahead of him and recognized it to be the outline of one of the habs. It didn't matter which one it was, as either had an airlock. "Thank you, Lord," Scott sighed with relief. He continued on to the airlock of the structure, but as he approached, a frightening realization crashed into his mind. He couldn't open the airlock while holding onto Diff. Hesitant, he started to put her down, when he heard Pierre's voice in his head set. "Turn right and come to the eastern hab. I'm holding the door open."

"Yes!" Scott exulted as he turned and made his way to the hab. Its outline was easily discernable, but otherwise dim through the dusty smog. Approaching it, he could just make out Pierre's form standing outside the structure and holding the airlock door wide open. Scott rushed into the airlock with Diff, willing himself to wait for Pierre to close the door before he opened the door to the inside of the hab. Finally, he was within, laying Diff on the nearest cot and swiftly removing her helmet.

He hardly noticed that Pierre had come through the airlock after him and was now peering over his shoulder. "Is she okay?" Scott had been so intent upon helping Diff that he was surprised by Pierre's voice.

"I hope so," Scott answered, trying not to show his disgust.

"I am . . . uh," Pierre was sheepish.

"Later, Pierre." Scott's voice was firm as he continued to attend to Diff. "For now, we need to help Diff. Have you contacted Terra Nova?"

"No. I waited to see if you and Diff made it."

Scott kept working on Diff. "Try to reach them now. I'm going to remove the rest of Diff's suit, and see if she's still alive."

Scott did not wait to see if Pierre would follow his orders, but kept removing the pieces of Diff's spacesuit. Then he felt for her pulse. It was weak, but definitely there. He watched for the rise and fall of her chest, and was relieved to see that she was breathing softly. "Diff, we made it. Diff wake up. Diff, are you okay?" Anguished, Scott bowed his head. Dieffenbachia Bateman was still unconscious, and Scott had never felt so helpless. *What can I do to help her?* He prayed. Aloud, he asked, "Pierre, have you got Terra Nova?"

"Yes," answered Pierre. "Tony is standing by."

Scott rose and scrambled to the com-link. "Tony, we need advice from Dr. Temple right away."

"I've already sent for her," Tony affirmed. "She should be here any second. Are we ever glad to hear from you. We called and called, and when there was no answer, we feared the worst."

"We were caught in the storm, but Pierre and I are fine," Scott assured him. "I don't know about Diff."

"Here's Damaris now."

"Scott, it's Damaris. What happened to Diff?"

Scott related the story of how Diff had fallen and punctured her suit. "She's breathing and has a weak pulse, but she won't wake up. Her knee is swollen too, but that can wait."

"Do you know how low the pressure got before you repaired her suit?"

"No." Scott hesitated. "I'm pretty sure I got it patched before all of her pressurization was gone, but I don't know how protected she was. I also don't know how much air she had after I repaired the hole. She lost a lot of air."

"You did everything you could, Scott. Watch her closely, and report any changes."

"I'm bringing her in to Terra Nova. She needs an exam and access to medical equipment. She may not have much time."

"Negative," he heard Rod respond.

"We have an emergency vehicle here that I can fly," argued Scott.

"Not in a Martian dust storm, you can't," Rod argued back. "Even if the wind wouldn't toss the craft, you have hardly any visibility. You can't see to take off or land. You will stay put and monitor Diff's condition with Damaris by com-link. We all care about Diff, but we can't risk losing both of you."

Scott's massive shoulders caved in, as he admitted to himself that Rod was right. He put his face in his hands, but couldn't hold back tears of frustration.

Damaris assured him, "We will all pray for Diff, Scott. That will help her more than anything I can do."

"I want to believe that," Scott's voice rasped, "but why would God let this happen? He could have prevented it."

"We often don't understand why things happen, Scott. But we know that God loves us, and He is faithful, and we can trust him to do what is best for Diff. I promise that I will be no more than 2 minutes away from the com-link until this is over."

"But what can I do to help her?" Scott wondered. "I'm a pilot—not a doctor. What about food and water? Won't she get dehydrated if she stays unconscious and we can't get her to drink?"

"You may be able to force water into her mouth. Try to get her to take water often," directed Damaris. "I'm praying that she'll gain consciousness before long. How's the coloring in her face?"

"She looks pale, but she always looks pale."

"Does her skin look bluish?"

"No, I don't think so."

"That's good, Scott," Damaris encouraged. "It sounds as if she is getting enough oxygen, and that means she is breathing. Now get the external thermometer out of your medical kit, and read her temperature."

Scott started to get up to find the medical kit, but Pierre beat him to it. He quickly handed the thermometer to Scott. Scott placed it on Diff's forehead and read, "It's 33.9 degrees Celsius. Isn't that too cold?"

"No, it's perfect," answered Damaris. "That external reading relates almost exactly to 37 internally, which is perfectly normal. Diff's signs are good right now. Monitor her, and call me immediately if her condition changes at all. I'll be nearby, and I'll check with you every hour around the clock. I also want you to get some instant ice out of your first aid kit and apply it to her swollen knee. Then you and Pierre take off your spacesuits, eat and drink something, and relax. All of you have been through an ordeal, and you need to rest and recoup. The pod has everything you need, so stay inside until this is over."

"All right, Doc, but the minute this storm stops, I'm bringing Diff in on the airplane we've got here."

"I agree, Scott." There was arguing from Rod in the background, but Damaris overruled him. "It's a medical decision, Rod. Dieffenbachia needs to be brought in. Pierre can wait in the hab alone for the few hours it will take Scott to fly in and back again. He'll be safe as long as he doesn't wander out alone."

Scott felt drained as he turned off the com-link and gazed at Diff, whose petite form had not moved. She looked so beautiful and helpless lying there that his heart ached. He put the ice on her knee and numbly began to remove his spacesuit, aware that Pierre was nervously standing by. "You heard the Doctor, Pierre. Make yourself at home."

"I can't," answered Pierre. "I let you both down, leaving you behind like that. You must hate me more that I hate myself."

"I don't hate you, Pierre, but I'd be lying if I told you I'm not mad at you. How could you leave Diff like that?"

"I don't know. I got scared, and all I could think of was getting to safety. I was terrified that the dust would hide everything, and I would be lost forever. I couldn't even think straight. It was like something took over my mind and body, and I just had to keep moving. I am so sorry, and I can never forgive myself."

Hearing Pierre, Scott was reminded that he had been recently forgiven by God, and he realized that his attitude toward Pierre was wrong. Had Pierre's behavior been any worse than his? "I forgive you, Pierre," he said, and he really meant it.

CHAPTER 17

RECOVERY

The next sol, Scott was jolted awake as Pierre shook him. "Scott, wake up!"

Still half asleep, Scott mumbled, "Diff?"

"Diff is still the same, but the wind has died down. Get up now!"

Scott's eyes sprang open, and he leaped to the tiny porthole of the hab. Pierre was right! The wind had blown itself out and the dust-laden air was clearing. Pierre had already made contact with Terra Nova, and Scott heard him talking with Tony. "Get Dr. Temple and Rod right now. The sky is clearing here, and we want to make sure it is at Terra Nova also. Scott and I must get Diff transported before the conditions change."

"Things are calm here too," came Tony's welcome reply. "There are still dust particles suspended in the atmosphere, but it's getting better. Rod ought to be coming in any second, and he can fill us in on visibility. As soon as the weather settled, he went out to the runway to check on it. I've called him back in. Here's Damaris."

"Scott, Pierre, how is the patient?" Damaris asked.

"There's been no change," Pierre's worried voice answered. "We've managed to get some water down her throat, but not nearly enough. We need to transport her to Terra Nova now."

Standing by impatiently, Scott decided to take action. He began rounding up all the pieces for Diff's spacesuit, knowing that he and Pierre would have to put her in it before they could take her outside to the airplane. Having second thoughts about putting her back into the damaged suit, he grabbed her spare one from the connecting tube. Vaguely, he heard Rod's voice in the background over the com-link.

"Visibility isn't the best, but I'm sure Scott's landed in worse conditions on Earth. We'll have a crew at the runway with lots of lights to help guide him in as well. I've contacted Hope, and Brian says the storm has moved past our area, and it isn't growing in size right now. Dust storms can blow back fast or grow huge with very little warning, so be quick. Pierre, I don't need to warn you to stay indoors while you are there alone, do I?"

"Don't worry, Commander. I'm no hero. I'll stay inside and read while I'm here alone."

"All right," Rod sounded resigned. "Get Diff in here ASAP."

"We're on it," responded Pierre. "Over and out." Turning to Scott, Pierre said, "I've checked the fuel level in the airplane, and it is good to go. I'm no pilot, so I couldn't very well do a preflight check, but everything looks okay to me from an engineering standpoint."

"Thanks, Pierre. Fuel is the main thing. I'll do the rest. Can you help me get Diff into this suit?"

"Right." Pierre and Scott carefully fitted the unconscious woman into the suit. At one point, she groaned, and they hoped she was waking up, but she didn't. Next, they fitted the helmet onto the suit and snapped it into place. They added a fresh life support system. Last, they donned their own suits and carried Diff out to the waiting emergency vehicle.

Scott held her in his arms while Pierre opened the cockpit. Then Scott climbed the ladder, carefully hoisting his precious burden into the back seat and fastening her in. Turning to the plane's computer, he programmed the craft to spread its folded wings. The tucked-in wings gracefully unfurled, and climbing down, he did a quick examination of the control surfaces and wheels, feeling confident that everything was in good condition. Turning to Pierre, he sensed a moment of camaraderie. "Thanks for your help, Pierre. I won't waste time. As soon as I'm sure Diff is in the Doctor's care, I'll head back. Round trip shouldn't take more than about two hours."

"Take all the time you need," answered Pierre. "I'll be okay inside."

Scott climbed back into the cockpit and lowered its cover. Turning on his radio, he called Terra Nova. "Terra Nova, this is Scott calling from the emergency craft."

"We read you, Scott," came Tony's voice. "We have everything ready on this end. Chang and Pavel are out at the runway and Damaris is standing by with an IV for Diff. Good luck."

Scott had never exactly flown the emergency aircraft, but he had mastered a simulator of the vehicle, so he was quite familiar with it. Still, this was real life, not a simulation. He concentrated on remembering the aircraft's unique characteristics. It would not have nor would it need a nice, long runway. It had been crafted to lift off the ground with rocket power and then shift that lifting power to propel it forward. The amazing craft wasn't really an airplane or a rocket, but sort of both. It was a lot like a Harrier jet from back at the turn of the century. Scott fired up the engines, looked at all of his controls, and knew that he was ready. Punching in the lift-off sequence, he was surprised at how gentle it was compared to lifting off of Earth. Once he achieved his desired altitude, he directed the craft forward toward Terra Nova. Visibility was not bad through the thin, orange fog. As Rod assumed, Scott had flown and landed in much thicker soup than this. *Thank you Lord, for clearing things up,* his thoughts soared.

Pierre watched the airplane leave with mixed emotions. He was glad that Diff was going to get medical help, but he was nervous about being alone, forty kilometers from everyone else. He watched until he could no longer see the craft, and then he reluctantly turned and trudged inside the pod.

Scott could not rely on a compass heading, since Mars did not have strong magnetic poles like Earth. Instead, a digital map readout, giving visual landmarks to guide the pilot, graced the instrument panel, and Terra Nova transmitted a radio signal for radar navigation. Scott was relying mostly on the homing beacon, because he was flying high to avoid the dust that still polluted the air at a lower elevation. With only forty kilometers to travel and a rocket powered airplane, he knew that he would reach the settlement in a matter of minutes. In fact, Chang's voice interrupted his thoughts.

"Come in Scott. This is Chang Lee."

"I read you loud and clear, Chang."

"We have you on our radar. You are almost to Terra Nova. Start your descent, or you will overshoot us."

"Roger that," answered Scott.

"You'll be coming in steep and fast. When the wheels touch down, stand on the brakes and deploy the parachutes. There are three of them. We have lights on for you, so you should have no trouble seeing us through the haze."

"I see you now," marveled Scott, noticing the luminescent rectangle in the distant terrain. He programmed in the sequence for descending, and angled down, aiming for the lighted runway before him. It had been less than ten minutes since he left Red City, and Scott was silently grateful that he didn't have to make this trip in the bouncy transport vehicle. The ground rose to meet him rapidly, and he leveled the nose of the airplane. The wheels screeched down at 150 miles per kilometer, and Scott stomped on the brakes, releasing the parachutes at the same time. As they opened, the entire airplane jolted from the sudden drag. The Terra Novan ridges loomed large in front of Scott, as the craft skidded to a stop with little runway to spare. Under other circumstances, the pilot might have enjoyed the thrill of the landing.

The plane had barely stopped, when he popped the cockpit cover. Relieved to see the ground crew approaching to help him with the airplane and Diff, he climbed out, stood on the ladder, and lifted Diff out of her seat before descending.

Chang and Pavel rushed forward lugging a stretcher. "Lay her on this," suggested Chang. "We can carry her faster and with less jostling than the terra-rover."

"That's for sure," agreed Scott, gently placing Diff on the stretcher. He barely put her down, when Chang and Pavel started for the pods. Within five minutes, they were inside the airlock, not stopping to remove their protective suits until they had safely delivered Diff to Dr. Temple. Scott followed close behind them.

Damaris had a bed ready, and she and Sandy carefully removed Diff's spacesuit and transferred her from the stretcher. Sandy immediately inserted an IV into Diff's arm to get nutrients and liquid into her. Then she asked Scott to help wheel the bed back into the women's pod. Damaris and Sandy planned to take turns giving Diff around the clock supervision there.

Scott knew he had done all he could and he should get back to Red City, but he was hesitant to leave. He longed to stay with Diff. As Damaris examined Diff, Sandy dragged him to the cafeteria. She poured him a cup of coffee and directed him to sit down and take off his helmet and gloves.

"Scott, I want you to relax a few minutes before you head back to Red City. Pierre will be fine until you get there."

"I know. I'm not worried about Pierre. I'm worried about Diff."

Sandy smiled at the gentle giant. "You've done everything you can for Diff. Now you have to leave her with us and trust God. I promise you we will do our best for her. I don't know why she's still unconscious, but dehydration is no longer a fear."

"What if she doesn't ever wake up?" Scott was anguished.

"I don't want you to think like that, Scott. You can't help her by worrying. The Lord commanded us not to worry in the book of Matthew.

> *Therefore I tell you, do not worry about your life, what you will eat or drink; or about your body, what you will wear. Who of you by worrying can add a single hour to his life? Seek first his kingdom and his righteousness, and all these things will be given to you as well."*

"But Sandy," argued Scott, "Diff isn't a believer. She's not ready to die."

"Then trust God, because He loves her, and He knows the condition of her soul. Let's pray right now together asking for God's help."

Immediately, the two bowed their heads together and prayed earnestly for their friend, also asking for wisdom for Damaris and peace for Scott.

An hour later, Scott reattached his helmet and gloves and drug his feet all the way out to the runway. Chang and Pavel had the plane refueled and the parachutes stowed. Chang pulled Scott aside to give him a few instructions.

"You know there is no runway at Red City, Scott."

"I know. I've flown this plane on a simulator many times, and I know it has the ability to land unconventionally. I've practiced landing over and over, so I should have no problems touching down. The biggest difficulty will be finding the site."

"That won't be a problem," Chang reassured. "Red City has a homing beacon, and Pierre has it turned on. Besides that, he says the visibility is excellent out there now. So just pay attention to your digital map and the beacon. You'll do fine."

"Promise me that someone will let me know right away if there is any change in Diff."

"We'll make sure you hear," promised Chang. "Rod is going to send Max and Jenny out in 3 sols. It cuts their time short, but he wants to bring you in and send you to Hope to relieve Brian. Diff's condition forced Rod's decision about who will pilot The Seeker back to Earth. It will be Brian. Both he and Dmitri need to spend a little time on the ground before traveling the next 14 months through space. So I'll be coming out to get you in Behemoth very soon."

"In what?"

"Behemoth," laughed Chang. "Andrew named the terra-rover Behemoth, and it seems to fit, so the rest of us have picked it up."

"That is a good name for it," smiled Scott. "I can't say I'm looking forward to the ride back in."

"It is a pretty rugged ride," Chang agreed. "However, we just can't afford to use up the amount of fuel that airplane requires for trips all the time. It's reassuring to have it for emergencies, but otherwise, it has to sit. We need the fuel we produce for the shuttle and the Orbiter."

"We need a plane that runs on solar power," Scott suggested.

"I've been saying that for the past couple of years," Chang agreed. "Solar or nuclear. Trouble is, no one has time. Pavel and I have a full time job just keeping everything we do have running. Andrew has been a great help, and as he learns more, I'm going to talk to Rod about letting us work on just such a contraption."

"You've got my vote."

Scott performed a pre-flight exam around the aircraft and climbed into the cockpit. Lowering the cover, he waved at the ground crew. They motioned that all was ready for take off. "See you soon," Scott promised into his headset.

The trip back to Red City proved just as fast as getting to Terra Nova. The visibility had improved immensely, so Scott was able to easily identify the landmarks indicated by the digital map. Since the dusty air had dissipated, he flew much lower going back, so he could see the rapid approach of Red City. *Now let's see if I can remember how to land this thing.*

Without a runway, the craft used retro-rockets for landing. That meant Scott had to slow it down and fire up the rockets at the same time. The retro-rockets were located on both sides of the fuselage, right under the wings. He powered them up, as he began to angle down. He wanted them up to full force by the time his altitude was 100 meters. At that point he would shut down the jet engines, and let the craft fall. The retro-rockets would keep pushing up with enough thrust to let the plane land gently. At least that was how it was supposed to work.

As he cut the jet engines, Scott's blood raced into overdrive. The craft plummeted in a free fall. He gave the retro-rockets more thrust that created the sensation of bouncing momentarily as the thrusting surge made contact with the ground. Scott gradually lowered the power, and the craft settled gently onto the ground. Breathing a sigh of relief, Scott looked around. He could see Red City, but he estimated he was a good 250 meters away from it. Scott's thoughts darkened, realizing that he and Pierre would have to pull the plane into its hangar. Suddenly he smiled as his thoughts brightened. *Wait until Behemoth arrives and let the mechanical monster pull the plane into the hangar.*

Finally, Scott deplaned and saw Pierre rushing out of the pod. He waved excitedly. *I've only been gone a couple of hours,* grinned Scott to himself. *You'd think he'd been alone for a week or two.*

"There's great news," Pierre's voice blasted into his headset. "Right after you left, Diff woke up. Damaris says she's weak, but talking. She remembers everything up until she lost consciousness."

Scott hastily closed the lid to the cockpit and raced to meet Pierre, his heart so full, he thought it would explode. He grabbed the surprised engineer and danced him around in a circle. "Praise God!" he shouted. Then he left a bemused Pierre standing outside as he crashed through the airlock to make contact with Terra Nova.

CHAPTER 18

SALVATION

For three sols, Diff progressed slowly back to normal, but showed impatience with being bedridden and waited upon. Dealing with inactivity was not something she was used to, and she anxiously wanted her life to get back to normal. Still, she couldn't deny that every time she tried to get up and walk around, the rounded walls seemed to oscillate wildly, forcing her back into her bunk. At least she was in the pod with the other women. She would have detested being curtained off in the entry module.

Sally had left earlier to help with communications for two hours, so Diff was alone with her disturbing thoughts. First, she was ashamed of her reaction to the dust storm, knowing that her foolish panic had nearly caused her death. Even worse, she had put Scott in danger as well. She tried to deny that he had helped her when Damaris first told her the story, but the truth was inescapable. Scott had risked his life in order to save her. How was she supposed to cope with that?

Dealing with Scott was minor, however, when placed against her promise to God. Dieffenbachia Bateman's memory was clear about her pledge, but she had no idea what to do about it. She had been waiting for the right moment to talk with Sandy Maloney, but Sandy wasn't around much. She was busy train-

147

ing people to take care of the plants in the greenhouse, since she was slated to travel home on The Seeker. Sandy had a husband patiently waiting on Earth. He had given his blessing for a two year stint on Mars, but he expected his wife back for good when her time was fulfilled, and she was anxious to head home. Sandy was a believer, probably the closest to a real, demonstrative Christian that Diff had ever known outside of Larraine. Diff wanted to discuss making a commitment to God with someone her own age. That left only Sandy that she knew well enough for such a personal matter.

"How is the patient?" Damaris asked, as she rapped on the doorway before entering.

"The patient is well and ready to go," grumped Diff. "I'm really sick of this bed rest thing. I've got to get back to work. Brian Delaney should be relieved on Hope."

"Not to worry," Damaris assured her. "He's enjoying rest and relaxation in Terra Nova as we speak."

"What do you mean?" Diff was alarmed.

"Rod sent Scott to take his place a couple of sols ago."

"But that's my job," Diff protested.

"Everyone knows that. Especially Scott," Damaris affirmed. "As soon as you are able, you will take over. However, your doctor says you aren't ready yet."

Diff angrily clambered out of her bunk. "I am ready. I'll show you ready," she argued. She no sooner had her feet placed firmly on the floor, when things started spinning and she plopped down again. Diff grimaced. "Maybe I'm not quite ready," she grudgingly admitted.

"Diff, no one is trying to take your job, least of all Scott. He was afraid you would take it personally, and he tried to get Rod to leave Brian up there until you were completely healed." Damaris felt like she was negotiating. "Still, I agree with Rod. Brian had to be relieved, and Scott is a perfectly good pilot. Scott wants to have responsibilities around here, just like everyone else. Besides, everyone knows you work too hard. It won't be easy for you, but I want you to relax for a change. Put your feet up and keep some ice on that sore knee. Read some good books, and get yourself back to full health. Admit it. You haven't really had a break for two years."

Diff sighed. "I suppose you're right. But I'm getting tired of just staying in this room in a bunk."

"I don't blame you," sympathized Damaris. "I want you to get up slowly, and I'll take you by the arm and walk you around in here for a few minutes. We'll schedule some walking several times a sol until you get back to normal. Larraine would love to help you out. There are also some great books you can access from the computer in here, and I strongly suggest you read a few."

Diff rose to her feet more carefully this time, and was delighted to find that the room was standing still. Damaris took her by the arm and they slowly made a circuit of the tiny pod. "More?" asked Damaris.

"Yes," said Diff. Being up and moving around was energizing. Even her sore knee felt better as she exercised it a little. After two more trips around the pod, Damaris helped her sit back on her bunk.

"What's going on with Sammy?" Diff wanted to know. "When I went out to Red City, he was still sick and waiting to go to Hope."

"Scott and Chang took him to the Orbiter. It's too early to know much yet, but I am hopeful that the environment away from the Martian dust will help him get well."

"What if it doesn't? There aren't any doctors on Hope. How will he get help if the dust isn't the problem?"

Damaris frowned. "If it isn't the dust, we're back to square one. He won't live much longer if he doesn't start breathing better. The best thing any of us can do at this point is pray for Sammy. Now you get some more rest, and look for something to read later."

An hour later, Sally Evanoff fairly bounced into the room, her bright blue eyes sparkling amid the fluffy, yellow hair that framed her face. Thirty-five years of age and climbing the fast track to success, Sally was now second in command at Terra Nova. She loved her job, and in the two years Diff had been here, she had never seen the biologist anything but optimistic.

"It's a beautiful sol out there," Sally began, "and everyone on base says to tell you to get well."

"I'm working on it, Sally," Diff agreed. "Can you tell me where Sandy is?"

"In the greenhouse, where else? Sandy's working hard against time to make sure we have a good crew to keep the plants healthy when she leaves. Our lives do depend on those plants, so she's right to take the training seriously. Unfortunately for her, she's working nearly around the clock on it. Hiro Tatsuda, as our resident horticulturist, will be in charge of the greenhouse when she leaves, with Larraine Temple to assist him."

"Is Larraine old enough for that responsibility?" asked Diff.

"She's almost eighteen, and a very serious girl. She also has a real gift for working with the plants, and she likes it," explained Sally. "Besides, over the past two years, Rod and I have worked closely with Sandy, so we know enough to support Larraine in this. We are confident that the greenhouse will thrive."

"When are you ever not confident?" teased Diff.

"Not very often," agreed Sally. "Trust me; the greenhouse will be in good hands. With my biology background, I know how important food is. Rod agrees, and he's anything but optimistic."

"You're right about that," laughed Diff.

The women's thoughts were interrupted by Sandy's voice from the connecting tube. "There is altogether too much levity in our pod."

Diff was happy to see Sandy coming through their door.

"We were just discussing the future of the greenhouse without Sandy Maloney, since our lives depend on that place for sustenance."

Sandy's plain face glowed with a smile that almost made her pretty. People usually thought of her as plain and mousy in appearance, but her loving and kind attitude more than made up for her looks. Everyone adored Sandy, and knew that she loved them back.

"Care of the greenhouse is under control. I guarantee it. If I had the least doubt, I'd call that husband of mine and tell him he'd have to hitch a ride to see me."

Diff and Sally both laughed, knowing that Sandy was excited about going home and anxious to see her husband, and there was no way she was staying on Mars when The Seeker left. They also knew she was dependable and would make sure that the greenhouse would flourish in her absence.

"I have to go to a meeting with Rod about our anticipated changes when The Seeker leaves for Earth," said Sally. "I'll see you two later."

"Who's going home?" asked Diff.

"Well, for sure we know that Brian Delaney will be the pilot. Sorry, Diff, but because of your accident, you're stuck here for another two years," teased Sally. "Also Dmitri Nazarov is slated, and Rod wouldn't dare keep him here another sol, the way he pines for his family. Then there's Sandy. It also looks as if Sammy will definitely be sent back to Earth. He's not going to make it if he stays here. There is room for two more on The Seeker, but right now there are no plans to send anyone else." Sally continued, "Rod and I are discussing the ramifications to Terra Nova. We still have two pilots, you . . ." she pointedly looked at Diff, "and Scott. Most of Dmitri's duties can be fulfilled by Preston Temple and Tony Davis. Larraine Temple is showing great promise in the greenhouse, although we all know it will be impossible to replace you, Sandy. With Sammy leaving, we'll still have a geologist here, but Rory sure does all he can to irritate Rod."

After her short visit, Sally left for her meeting with Rod, and Diff finally had her moment alone with Sandy. "Uh, Sandy," she began.

"Yeah?"

"I need to talk with you about my near tragedy."

Sandy looked up, wondering where Diff was headed. "I'm listening," she told her friend.

"Right before I blacked out, I promised that if God would rescue me, I would give Him my life," admitted Diff.

Sandy smiled. "That's wonderful!" she exclaimed.

"The trouble is," Diff continued, "I don't know how to do it. And I don't know how to know that I did it, when I do it. Besides that, how do I know that God is real, anyway?"

"He kept you alive, didn't he?" challenged Sandy.

"Well, from what I've heard, Scott kept me alive."

"Don't you see? God had Scott there. Pierre didn't care enough to help you. How many people would have risked their lives to help you? Scott stayed and helped. And God helped Scott know what to do and gave him the strength to do it."

Diff mulled those thoughts over in her mind, and could find nothing illogical about them. "I guess I could believe that. I sure never gave Scott any reason to want to help me."

Sandy sighed with exasperation. "Diff, can't you tell that Scott is in love with you? Everyone can tell, but that's beside the point. God provided a way for you to be saved. He also provided a way for you to be saved for eternity, and that's what we need to discuss now."

"Okay," agreed Diff. "I admit that I sure wasn't ready to die. I hate to say it, but I was terrified, and my behavior was embarrassing. I don't want to feel that way ever again."

"Everything I'm going to tell you is from the Bible, but it will make sense if you will keep your mind open," began Sandy.

"The Bible is God's Word, and from it we learn that we need to be saved and how to be saved."

"I'm listening."

Sandy warmed to her story. "In the beginning, God created everything, including mankind, flawless. But Adam and Eve gave into temptation, disobeying God, and separating themselves and mankind forever from God."

"I've heard the story of Adam and Eve," Diff shrugged. "I don't see how it applies to me."

"It applies, because it explains how sin came into the world. Have you ever known anyone who doesn't sin?"

"I guess not," agreed Diff.

Sandy continued. "Since God is perfect, He cannot look on sin. Does that make sense?" she asked.

"Yes," answered Diff, "but since everybody sins, what hope is there?"

"You are asking exactly the right question," smiled Sandy. "There is no way that people can earn their way back to God, because He can't look on our sin. So God made a plan, and it is such a wonderful, simple plan that many people think it's too easy, and they won't believe it."

"Well, what's the plan?" Sandy had Dieffenbachia Bateman's complete attention.

"God sent his Son, Jesus, into the world. While he was here, Jesus lived life just like we do. He experienced everything we do, all the desires, temptations, and hurts. But he never sinned. He lived a perfect life."

"Even if that's true, I don't see how it helps me," said Diff honestly.

"God's plan was that Jesus would live a perfect life and then become a perfect sacrifice for anyone who would accept it. Jesus was put to death for my sin, and your sin, and the whole world's sin. He died so that we can live."

"How can his dying allow me to live?" questioned Diff.

"God offers Jesus as a sacrifice for your sins. All you

have to do is accept his gift. When you do, your sins are for-given. They are covered by the blood of Christ Jesus, and you have a perfect relationship with God."

"That sounds too easy," protested Diff.

"The formula is easy, but sometimes it isn't so easy to confess sins and ask Jesus to forgive."

"Sandy, are you telling me that all I have to do is admit my sins and ask Jesus to forgive me?" Diff was truly seeking.

"Yes, that's all," affirmed Sandy. "Do you want to do it?"

"I do want to belong to God, and I promised that I'd give my life to Him. Can you help me say the right words?"

Sandy carefully laid it out. "Here is what you have to do. You should pray, thanking God that He made a way for you to be saved. Then confess your sins. You don't have to name every single one–who could possibly remember them all–but if there are some that come to mind, name them. Then ask Jesus to save you. Last, thank him for doing it. Do you think you can do all that?"

"I think so," answered Diff. "Help me if I don't do it right, okay?"

"I'll be right here, praying for you."

"Dear God," began Diff. "I'm doing this because I told you I would. Thank you for saving my life and giving me the chance to do this. Thank you for making a plan for me, so I could be saved. I have done many bad things in my life. I'm sure you remember sins I've committed that I've forgotten. I've been selfish and mean and only cared about myself. Please forgive my sins. Thank you that Jesus died so my sins could be forgiven. I accept your gift of his supreme sacrifice for me. Thank you for hearing my prayer and saving me. Amen."

Diff looked up into Sandy's hazel eyes, which were flooded with tears. Sandy hugged her, congratulating her on making the best decision of her life.

"I don't really feel any different," Diff said in a worried tone of voice.

"It's not about feelings. God promises that if you accept His gift, you are forgiven and saved. You can trust God to do what He says. He's perfect, and He can't lie."

"I can accept that," agreed Diff, as a warm feeling flowed inside her. Then she frowned at her painful thoughts. "Since God has forgiven me, I need to forgive someone else."

"Who would that be?"

"I've been holding a grudge against Scott for the past couple of years. I should tell him that I forgive him, but he isn't here any more."

Sandy had the solution. "I work the com-link tonight from midnight until 2 AM. You can come into the communications center and talk to him then."

"I don't think I can walk that far without help."

"I could get Larraine to come help you. Would that be okay with you?"

Diff agreed. "That would be great. In the meantime, I'm supposed to find a good book to read on the computer. Do you know if the Bible can be accessed online?"

"It sure can," confirmed Sandy. "That would definitely be a good book for you to read. I recommend starting with the book of John."

It was just a little before midnight when Larraine lightly rapped on the door to the women's pod. Sally was sound asleep after a grueling 16 hours of work, and no one wanted to disturb her. Larraine tip-toed over to Diff's bunk, and the joy-filled woman quickly sat up. Having made the decision to contact Scott hours ago, she could hardly wait. Grabbing Larraine's offered arm, she cautiously stood and waited a moment to be sure there was no vertigo. Then together they slowly walked through the tube that connected the pod to the communications center.

When they arrived, Sandy was alone at the com-link. She sat Diff down and said, "Are you sure you want to do this?"

"I'm sure."

"Then I'll call Hope and leave the rest up to you."

"Thanks," responded Diff.

Sandy opened the link. "Terra Nova to Hope. Come in please."

Hoping to reach Scott, the three women were disappointed to hear Chang's cheerful voice chirp, "What's up Terra Nova? Besides you, Maloney, of course."

Sandy groaned. "Can't you ever be serious, Chang? Let me talk with Scott."

"No can do. Scott is having his beauty sleep," explained Chang. "He can't talk right now, or he will turn into an ugly alien ogre."

Frustrated, Diff grabbed the com-link from Sandy. "Chang, this is Dieffenbachia Bateman. Let me talk to Scott, or I will make your life miserable when I replace him on Hope."

"Oohh, I am *so* afraid," mocked Chang. "All right. I'll get him, but it's not my fault if he doesn't like it. Do you know how big he is?"

Diff rolled her eyes, as the other two chuckled. "Did you notice how dull it's been around here since Chang left?" joked Larraine.

Sandy caught Larraine's eyes and motioned that they should give Diff privacy.

"Right," mouthed Larraine, in agreement.

Larraine and Sandy quietly left the communications area, so Diff could be alone. Diff appreciated their thoughtfulness, but she had no idea what to say to Scott. Apologizing had never been easy for her. She drummed her fingers on the desk as she waited impatiently. Finally she heard Scott's sleepy voice.

"Jamison here."

Diff hesitated, then took a deep breath and began, "Scott, it's me, Diff."

" . . . Diff?" Scott sounded very awake now. "Why are you calling me in the middle of the night?"

Diff closed her eyes and searched her mind for the right thing to say. "I'm sorry to wake you, but I wanted to thank you for saving my life."

"Anyone would have done that." Scott was embarrassed.

"Apparently not Pierre," quipped Diff, "but there's more than that. Something happened earlier to change my life." Diff paused, wondering if Scott would understand what she was talking about.

"Go on," coaxed Scott.

"I accepted Jesus as my Savior," admitted Diff.

Scott could hardly believe what he was hearing. He felt like jumping up and down and turning cartwheels, and that was physically impossible for the large astronaut. He could not stop the smile that connected both sides of his face.

Waiting for Scott to say something, Diff asked, "Did you hear what I said?"

"That's outstanding news, Diff. I am really, really happy for you. I recently did the same thing myself."

"You?" Diff was surprised.

"Yep," Scott enthused.

"Well anyway, I wanted to tell you that I'm sorry I've been so awful to you since you arrived, and I want you to know that I've forgiven and forgotten what you said to me."

"Praise the Lord," breathed Scott prayerfully.

"What?" asked Diff.

"Thank you, Diff. I'm so sorry for what I said. I never meant it. I was such a fool."

"Like I said, I've forgiven and forgotten. I'd like to be friends again, Scott. Could we do that?"

"Absolutely!" affirmed Scott.

"Okay. I have to sign off now. I'm not really supposed

to tie up the com-link with personal business. We'll talk more when I transfer to Hope to relieve you."

"I can't wait!" Scott's voice cracked with emotion, and Diff smiled, picturing her former friend in her mind.

"Terra Nova out," she said dreamily.

On Hope, Scott turned to see Chang's beaming face. "Well, I'll be," began the cheerful mechanical engineer.

"Don't start with me," warned Scott, frowning darkly.

Chang chuckled. "Oh, I'm not the one who's starting anything."

CHAPTER 19

GROWTH

It had been a week and a half since Dieffenbachia almost died in the Martian dust storm. She was feeling much better, which only served to make her more anxious to get back to work. She had to admit that she was truly learning about her new relationship with the Creator, and that was a good thing. Taking Sandy's advice, she read through the book of John in the New Testament. *Why has nobody ever told me this stuff before?* she wondered.

Diff found the stories of Jesus amazing. *Not stories—this is real,* she reminded herself. Jesus actually lived the way he told others to live. His concern for people showed through his teachings, actions, and his miracles. Her eyes filled with tears each time she reread chapters eighteen and nineteen. *How could anyone torture and kill a man who only went about doing good?* When that question popped into her mind, she reminded herself that her sins could only be forgiven through the death of Christ. *My sins killed him as sure as any people involved back then. It is so unfair, but thank you God.*

Reading on through the rest of John, Diff always felt the excitement of an incredible ending to a wonderful story. *I can't imagine how the disciples must have felt when they actually saw*

Jesus again, she thought to herself. *No wonder they changed the world forever.*

Diff also enjoyed her walks through the pods with Larraine. She really could manage by herself now, but having someone else nearby was reassuring, just in case. She also loved discussing her readings with someone who understood.

The shuttle was scheduled to take the Earthbound travelers to the Orbiter in a few sols, and Rod had promised that Diff would be on it to take over for Scott. Red City was out of the question, because Rod wasn't sure she was physically up to it. But he also knew she was ready for a change of scene and more responsibility. Hope would be a good place for her to hang out while she recovered completely.

Diff enthusiastically welcomed going to Hope. She always enjoyed its quietness and loved running on its track. She believed the exercise would really help her get back to 100 percent. Besides, Chang was fun to work with, and his great attitude rubbed off on those he was near. Not only that, she had to admit that she wanted to see Scott.

Larraine arrived already dressed in her pressurized suit and then stood by ready to help while Diff donned hers. They were meeting Preston Temple at the life support recycling center. Pres would be the person most responsible for overseeing the center while Diff manned the Orbiter, and there were some details that she wanted to go over with him. "You know," she told Larraine, "I could go by myself."

"I know you could, Ms. Bateman," responded Larraine, "but this gives me the chance to be with you a little more before you leave for three months, and perhaps I can even learn a little chemistry by listening to you and my dad."

Diff sighed. "Larraine, I've told you before, call me Diff just like everyone else. I don't like this Ms. Bateman stuff."

"But you're one of my teachers," the student protested. "I'm supposed to be respectful of adults."

Diff laughed. "You are respectful, Larraine, and I appreciate it. However, we are a family up here, and no one goes by titles, except perhaps Rod. Please just call me Diff."

"I'll try, but it might be hard for me at first."

"That's okay. I'll keep reminding you."

As usual, it was a sunny but shrouded sol, as the two made their way into the out of doors. The older woman was elated to find that she could maneuver very well by herself in her pressurized suit, while the younger woman conscientiously stood by to assist. They both ambled out to the recycling center at the end of the landing strip.

Along the northeast side of the landing strip, in a direct route from the center straight to the greenhouse, lay piping to transport the air to the modules. Programmed robots constantly read the data about the quality and amount of air and pressure directed to the settlement. Any drop in pressure, no matter how small, resulted in an alarm. If an alarm sounded, a robot automatically shut off the air from one of the recyclers and started it flowing from the other. Since air is critical to life, Terra Novans practiced failure drills. So far the system had worked flawlessly, but everyone knew the potential for problems existed.

Preston had already been reviewing the data at the site for the past hour, and he informed the arriving Diff that everything was working well. "This is an amazing concept," he said. "Whoever thought of this process should have received the Nobel Prize for science."

"That's for sure," agreed Diff. "Without it, we couldn't have a settlement on Mars. Can you imagine trying to transport all the air we need from Earth?"

Preston shook his head, even though the movement inside his helmet wasn't obvious to the other two. "There's no way," he commented.

"Are you up to speed on all of this?" asked Dieffenbachia. "Do you have any last minute questions?"

"No, I understand the process and my responsibility," Preston assured her.

"Great," said Diff. "Rod and Sally can help you out with any problems too. So I'm not worried." Suddenly amazed at herself, Diff realized how much she had changed. In the past, she found it difficult to relinquish any of her responsibilities, erroneously believing that no one else could do them as well as she. Now she knew better. Part of her comfort existed in knowing that God, and not Dieffenbachia Bateman, was in charge. *Imagine that!* she thought to herself. *Who would have ever thought that I would understand that? I really am a different person.*

At the same time, Scott was circling Mars and gazing at a distant blue dot from the viewing port of Hope. After more than a week in the Orbiter, the astronaut never tired of looking out at the heavens. The view appeared incredibly different than that observed from the surface of Mars. On Mars, annoying fines almost always hovered in the atmosphere, making a clear view of the heavens rare. Usually the only visible star was the Sun, and Scott didn't count that as a star, even though it was. Orbiting above the Martian atmosphere gave him a new perspective, and his new relationship with the Creator was even more exciting. *To think that I never realized Your genius and creativity before,* Scott praised with fascination.

The blue dot that captured his attention was Earth. So distant, yet it was comforting to be able to see it and know that there were millions of people on that distant world. *I wonder if any of them are looking up here at us right now?*

Chang was a pro at the operations on the Orbiter and also a good teacher. He was even more spirited than usual, realizing that for a change, he knew more about the Orbiter than the pilot on-board. The two men enjoyed becoming acquainted and had each gained the respect of the other.

Orbiting, Hope progressed through several sols and nights during the 24 Martian hours that made one sol and night on the ground. That in itself was a fantastic experience, and Scott loved seeing so many sunrises and sunsets in each orbit. But his favorite thing had to be the sky while the Orbiter passed through darkness. It was so black. Amazingly, the darkness was spattered with beautiful, bright, intermittent points of light. So many stars glistened in the clear outer space that it was difficult to discern the constellations. On Earth, light pollution hid many objects in the night sky from view. Now Scott enjoyed a radically different scene.

The Orbiter actually ran itself for the most part. The people aboard monitored its altitude, and had the capability of firing engines to change its orbit if needed. That occurrence would be an unusual event, and it had never happened yet. Orbiting astronauts also monitored the weather on the surface of Mars. Just as Brian had warned Terra Nova of the impending dust storm, those aboard Hope were the first to notice a change in the Martian surface weather. This being the end of the summer season in the southern hemisphere, Scott and Chang had seen many small swirling dust storm areas in that section of the planet. So far, none had threatened to travel into the northern area or engulf the planet. Still, they kept their eyes on the little storms, knowing the potential for a planet-wide tempest.

Just like Diff, Scott spent time reading the Bible. He decided to begin at Matthew and read through the entire New Testament online. By now, he had completed the first two books and was surprised to find himself familiar with most of what he read. He had heard it in Sunday School as a child. He had never understood much of it before, and he was now looking at the writings through new eyes. Surprised at his thirst for learning more, Scott absorbed several chapters a sol.

Even more surprising, Scott found himself wanting to share his discoveries with Chang. Chang humored him and listened but had no interest in believing. "I'm glad it makes you happy, Scott, but I have my own ideas. I'm a good person, and I think people just need to do their best and treat others right."

He really is a good person, Scott agreed. *I like Chang,*

and that's all the more reason for me to share God's Word with him.

The two men anxiously anticipated hosting those returning to Earth. There was plenty of room in the Orbiter, and the thought of seeing the others gave them something to look forward to. Rod had informed them earlier that sol that Diff would be on the shuttle to serve her stint. Scott anticipated seeing her for two whole sols before he flew the shuttle back to Terra Nova and then traveled out to the drilling site. He could hardly wait.

Has she really forgiven me? It seems unbelievable. The time he could spend with Diff would be short, but Scott believed it would be his best two sols of the past two years. He hoped that they could start anew and put the past behind them. Scott surprised himself when he realized that sharing his faith with Diff was more important than anything right now. Knowing that believing was something they had in common thrilled him. Scott started to make plans, because he didn't want to waste a minute of the time they had together.

CHAPTER 20

INSUBORDINATION

Three sols later, Rory Galveston gulped down a quick breakfast of applesauce and coffee. At least two hours before solbreak, the cafeteria was vacant, and he hurried. So far everything was going according to plan.

Rory fumed. Ever since he had taken Larraine and Andrew to the cave, Rod had effectively grounded him. The commander blamed Rory for Andrew's accident, and had forbidden him to take the Temple kids there again. Besides that, he was enforcing his rule that Rory couldn't go alone. Rory had done everything short of throwing a tantrum, but the commander was standing firm. To Rory, it even seemed that Rod was taking a twisted delight in keeping him Terra Nova bound. Rod insisted that no one in the settlement could be spared to spend a sol at the cave with the geologist. To top it off, Rod kept needling him to go out to Red City. *My job is to discover—not help drill,* the geologist arrogantly reminded himself.

Taking a closer look at the silo-like shaft where they almost lost Andrew became an obsession. The smooth, glassy appearance intrigued him, and he wanted to examine it under normal rather than emergency conditions. Could it be a form of obsidian? If so, then he and Sammy were probably correct in their thinking that the ice cap was covering up a dormant volcano. It would also be interesting to see if he could determine how deep the shaft went and whether it might be a conduit to more tunnels within the cave. *I refuse to stay on base any longer,* Rory's rebellious thoughts surfaced. *Whether Rod knows it or not, the cave could be scientifically critical to Terra Nova. It still holds the promise of signs of life, but beyond that, UNSEF has long held the belief that caves could provide great protection and housing for Martian explorers. Rod Sherman is preventing the study of something important to Terra Nova, just because he has a grudge against me.* Rory finished his coffee, and his thoughts. *I'm through being the brunt of Rod's unhappiness. He should take a long leave back on Earth. His conservative attitude is slowing down Terra Nova's progress.*

"Good morning, Dr. Galveston."

Rory jumped guiltily, as the voice from behind him startled him. Turning around, he was relieved to see Larraine Temple. She wasn't someone who could keep him from going.

"What are you doing up, Larraine?" asked the surprised geologist.

"I'm supposed to report to the greenhouse at 8 A.M. this morning."

"It's only 5 A.M. right now," suggested Rory.

"I know, but I've been awake for awhile. I'm pretty nervous about my responsibilities in the greenhouse, I guess. Anyway, I decided to just get up, since I can't sleep. I thought I'd get some coffee and do some studying out here."

Rory hadn't noticed before that Larraine was carrying her handheld computer. *Cute,* was the word that entered his mind as he viewed her tousled blonde hair and slender frame inside the hot pink jumpsuit. Larraine was probably the one person on base who appreciated what Rory was studying. Not only that, she was intelligent, interesting, and seemed to genuinely care about others. *Too bad she's not about four years older,* thought the young scientist.

"What are you doing up?" Larraine asked Rory.

"Well, I couldn't sleep either, so I thought I'd get an early start on the sol. I have a lot of soil and rock analysis to take care of." Rory's eyes shifted away, as he found it difficult to lie, even for a good reason.

Larraine's green eyes seemed to bore right through him as she smiled. "I don't believe you," she said. "I think you're going out to the cave."

Rory's face reddened, almost proving his guilt, but he refused to affirm the truth of Larraine's guess. "I'm not allowed to go to the cave by myself," he argued.

"I know," agreed Larraine, "but you are going, aren't you?"

Silence echoed through the cafeteria, as Rory mentally prepared his excuses. "I have to go," Rory pleaded. "Rod has kept me here for weeks with nothing to do. There is a wealth of information in that cave. Information that can energize the development of Terra Nova. Information that will lead to important scientific discovery."

"I agree with you, but I can't agree with breaking Rod's rules to go out there alone."

"Well, what do you think I should do?" Rory was frustrated.

"I don't know," admitted Larraine. "I'd probably start by praying about it."

Rory laughed, as he couldn't believe what he was hearing. "Well, I wouldn't. I don't even believe in God, and if I did, I don't think a supreme being would be all that concerned with whether or not I go exploring in a cave. No. I think I should just get out there before Rod realizes I'm gone. Once I'm out there, what can he do? And maybe I'll find something to prove to him that I should be allowed to carry on some research out there."

"It's dangerous to be exploring on Mars by yourself. Even you told Andrew that."

"Andrew is eleven years old."

"Do you really believe it's safe for you to go by yourself?"

Rory sighed, "Larraine, I know there are good reasons for the rule that you shouldn't go exploring by yourself. Yet do you think it's fair for Rod to keep me away from the cave forever? Sometimes a person has to take a risk. We wouldn't even be on Mars if there weren't people willing to take risks. Do you think getting to Mars was a safe thing? Do you think we're safe in Terra Nova? Nothing about this is safe."

Larraine knew that Rory's opinions about safety were right-on. Living on an alien planet was far from safe. Conversely, she also knew that what he was planning to do pushed the limits. Still, she found it hard to argue with him. And she agreed that Rod seemed to be treating him unfairly. It wasn't Rory's fault that Andrew fell into the shaft. If anything, it was hers. She should have been paying better attention to her little brother. She knew what he was like.

"You aren't going to tell anyone, are you?" Rory's attractive brown eyes pleaded with her.

How can anyone say no to him? wondered Larraine. Her heart took over her mind as she heard herself say, "I won't tell anyone where you are as long as they don't ask about you, but I won't lie for you."

"Thanks," said Rory. "I'm off to the robot shed to grab N3. Then I'll be out of here before anyone else is up. Rod probably won't even miss me."

With that, Rory carried his dishes to the microwave cleaner and hastily departed. Approaching the tunnel, he turned, smiled at Larraine, revealing his left cheek dimple, and put his finger to his lips in the "shhh" sign. Then he disappeared through the passageway.

Larraine experienced mixed emotions. She knew she had developed a crush on the young, handsome scientist, and felt pleased that he trusted her with his secret. However, she also knew he was in the wrong. *Is it dishonest for me to keep it to myself? Am I compromising, because I like him so much?* Larraine argued with herself. *That dimple in his cheek is so cute.*

No—nothing about Rory is cute. He's gorgeous. I know he's too old for me now, but maybe in a couple of years, he won't be. Larraine smiled at her thoughts. Then she frowned, wondering if she was doing the right thing by letting him go.

Within thirty minutes, Rory had attached a wagon to N3, loaded with every tool he could think of that might be required and more air tanks than he could possibly need. He'd prove to Rod that exploration could be accomplished alone. He also trampled another Terra Novan rule, as he took N3 without signing for the rover. Rory was not going to leave clues to his whereabouts behind. He didn't want anyone to know that N3 was with him. Chances were, N3 wouldn't be missed before he came back in the evening anyway.

Rory knew he would be hungry before he returned, but at least NASA had long ago provided a way for astronauts in pressurized suits to have a snack. Inside the helmet, reachable by mouth, was a storage compartment for energy bars. Edible wrapping made it possible for the person inside the suit to eat. Water was also accessible through a straw inside the helmet. He'd be hungry before he returned, but not starving.

Opening the door of the shed, Rory saw that it was still dark out. *You shouldn't be going out alone in the dark,* Rory's thoughts troubled him. *It's the only way I can get out of here,* he reminded himself. *Yes, but you can't see where you are going. You could trip and fall,* argued his mind. *I'll be careful,* Rory promised himself. N3 was equipped with a small headlight that operated by battery at night, so by walking beside the rover, Rory's pathway lit up dimly. Still, the geologist recognized the need to travel slowly and carefully until the sun rose. He didn't mind, because he figured there was still at least an hour before Terra Novans would be rising. He would be long gone before anyone was likely to miss him.

It took longer than usual, but Rory approached the cave just at sunrise. The bright rays of the sun reflected off the ochre walls of the ridge, accentuating the gaping, black cavity in its wall. The darkness drew Rory in, prompting him to hurry to the portal. He moved N3 as near as he could and then detached the wagon from it. He planned to leave the wagon, loaded with tools, in the cave for future exploring, so he would not have to continually pack the same items back and forth from the settlement. "Now be a good rover, and wait here," he ordered N3.

Once inside the cave, the first thing Rory did was hammer a piton into the side of the cave near the tunnel, making sure it held solidly. He tied one end of a rope through it, and the other end of the rope around his waist, being extremely cautious. Rory had packed five lanterns and all kinds of tools in the wagon, including many more pitons. Mountain climbers back on Earth used pitons to help them scale steep cliffs, and they were the perfect tool to help secure Rory to the wall of the cave while he explored. He had also piled four bundles of rope onto the wagon, each 50 meters long. He planned to stop and install pitons every time he ran out of rope, attaching new rope to the spike and himself. *I'll show Rod that exploring can be accomplished safely solo,* he smugly thought to himself. Then Rory strenuously wheeled the heavily laden wagon into the beckoning tunnel.

Carrying a sixth, lighted lantern and using all his strength, Rory lugged the wagon up the incline of the tube that ended at the silo. The exertion made him stop and rest a few minutes, as he looked around and planned his next move. First, he installed another piton, releasing the former rope from his waist and attaching a new one to himself and the nearby support. Once he was securely attached, he lit three more lanterns and carefully spaced them around the ledge that overlooked the chasm. He stopped to look around, realizing that in the excitement of Andrew's accident, he had not been able to investigate anything. Remembering the faint impression of a glassy wall of rock, he was unprepared for the grandeur of what he was now seeing. The entire wall was smooth and glossy, reflecting the light and increasing its effect dramatically. The space glowed with an unreal beauty, and Rory savored it. He chipped off a piece of the wall and put it in his tool case to take back to the base for analysis.

Next, Rory attached another lantern to one of his ropes. He gingerly lay down on the ledge and dropped the lantern over its edge, lowering it slowly and carefully. The smooth, curved walls glistened as the lantern made its way lower and lower. The lantern passed the small ledge that had saved Andrew, and Rory continued to lower it. He could still see no evidence of the end of the duct. Rory had almost come to the end of the rope, and he wanted to find the bottom of the tube, so he decided to tie another lantern onto the rope and attach another rope onto the second lantern. That way, he could continue to lower the first lantern, and get more light from the second as well.

The geologist continued lowering the lanterns. By the time he had come to the end of the second rope, he realized that the silo was deeper than he had imagined. There was still no bottom in sight. He also had seen no sign of any other ledges, and was amazed at how lucky Andrew had been to land on the one jutting edge that existed. He shuddered to think of the disaster had the young boy missed it.

Rory ran out of rope, so further exploration of the depths proved impossible. Even he was not about to detach himself from the safety of the piton to gain more rope. He now knew that the silo plummeted at least 100 meters deep. One hundred tubular meters of perfectly smooth glass. Such a geological specimen on Earth would be an incredible find. What could have caused it? Rory removed an electronic camera from his tool kit and began to take pictures. He wanted a record to prove to Rod the significance of the wondrous find.

After removing three more geological specimens from the silo, Rory stopped for a snack, relishing the luxury of the energy bar. Disappointed that he had found no evidence of any other passages in the cave, he imagined it was still likely that the cave jutted off at the bottom of the silo. He determined to explore the exterior and see if he could discover another entry somewhere. The lone explorer hoisted the lowered lanterns back up to the ledge, coiled the attached ropes, and packed everything onto the wagon. Once the wagon was loaded, he retraced his steps down the tunnel and back to the roomy entrance, leaving the remaining ropes attached to the two pitons.

After resting and attaching a fresh air tank, Rory decided to leave most of his equipment on the wagon inside the room, and he took only one rope, a lantern, and his tool kit. Reaching inside his tool kit, he removed his telescopic viewer. The specialized tool allowed a view similar to that provided by binoculars on Earth, but visible through the pressurized suit's face plate. Standing outside the cave entrance, he scanned the surrounding cliff walls. Rory saw no obvious opening anywhere, but he was not about to give up. Instead of heading for Terra Nova, the scientist explored behind the cloven wall, walking away from the cave. The land appeared relatively flat all the way to the ridge opposite the cave, but as he came nearer to that wall of rock, Rory could see that the land did not meet it.

Excitement grabbed the young geologist as he realized that the flat land upon which he stood, sharply dropped off about 25 meters before the upwardly jutting rampart before him. He carefully crawled up to the edge of the land and peered over the rim. In the light, he could see that he was looking into the depths of a yawning but narrow abyss. He aimed his telescopic viewer at the bottom, and was rewarded with the view of a huge hole in the wall directly below and under him. *I'll bet it connects with my silo,* he exulted, *but how can I get down there?*

Rory dejectedly knew there was no way to scale down the side of the cliff by himself. It would be a difficult, time-consuming endeavor, even with a group of people. Eventually it could and would be done. He snapped off some photos for proof and study, and reluctantly trudged back to N3.

Only now did Rory take the time to look at his geological specimens from the cave. In the light, their nearly translucent quality trapped a smoky gray color. Were they volcanic in origin? They certainly appeared so. Rory remembered that NASA had successfully experimented with extracting water from obsidian back on Earth, so he had potentially found a source of water. That should make Rod happy.

The young scientist again renewed his air supply. He hated to leave, but the sun perched low over the western horizon. *Where did the time go?* He would be pushing it to return to Terra Nova before nightfall, and he didn't relish the idea of traveling in the dark again. With what he had found, he was sure he'd have Rod's blessing to continue exploring out here, so he would leave it for another sol. His heart bursting with the thrill of discovery, he loaded his gear onto N3. Rory exulted, "Let's go home, Buddy."

CHAPTER 21

GREENHOUSE

While Rory explored, Larraine worked and learned all morning in the greenhouse. Sandy Maloney taught her all about the irrigation system. *I hope I remember everything,* Larraine thought to herself. The various plants were watered according to a schedule. Some required watering every sol, while others had to dry out before they were watered again. The young woman reminded herself that all living things need water. If something happened to the water supply, nothing living would last long.

There was so much to remember: when to plant, when to thin, when to fertilize, when to water, when to reap, temperature regulation. At least there were no weeds yet. That was pretty impressive. No weeds on Mars! The only plants existing here were those that settlers had brought from Earth.

"Let's go have lunch, Larraine." Sandy was ready for a break.

"That sounds good to me," replied Larraine. Not only feeling hungry, she looked forward to a break. It would be nice to relax for awhile.

Having returned by tunnel to the living center, the two grabbed sandwiches and juice in the cafeteria area and sat down to eat.

Beginning the conversation, Larraine asked Sandy, "Are you looking forward to going home?"

"I am so ready," Sandy affirmed. "This was an amazing opportunity for me, but I miss my husband and everything about Earth. I can't wait to go home."

"I wish I was going," Larraine commented wistfully.

"Do you really?"

"Well, sometimes I'm glad to be here. It is pretty exciting. I know it's important for the future, but I miss my friends and all the things we have on Earth. Maybe I like the greenhouse because it at least has some green living things in it."

"I know what you mean," laughed Sandy. "Mars is awfully primitive and bleak. On the other hand, it has a wild, unusual beauty, and we are lucky to be able to see it in person."

"That's true," agreed Larraine. "I like the people here too. Everyone depends on everyone else, and they all get along so well."

"Well, usually. Sometimes we get on each other's nerves too. It's hard to have to rely on others so much. I know it must be especially hard for you and Andrew, with no one else your age here."

Larraine smiled, remembering how difficult it was traveling in the confined space within The Seeker with five other people for seven months. It now struck her that the returning crew would spend twice as long returning to Earth. "Fourteen months in The Seeker. That's what you have to look forward to. How will you ever endure that?"

"It won't be easy," agreed Sandy. "Wouldn't it be nice if we could just propel ourselves in a straight line? Unfortunately, with everything in the Solar System moving, you can't shorten the times involved, at least not with our technology of the present."

"Why does it take twice as long to return to Earth as it did for us to get here?"

"Well, if we wanted to just stay here another year and

a half, it would only take seven months. But that adds more months onto our time away from Earth, and we can get back to Earth sooner than that by leaving now and flying by Venus for a gravity assist. So even though we spend more time in space traveling, we'll get home much sooner than if we wait."

"Are there still only four of you heading back to Earth?"

"Well, Rod's for sure sending me," grinned Sandy. "It looks like Sammy will go. Brian Delaney will pilot The Seeker, and Dmitri Nazarov has been promised a ride home. Beyond that, it's anyone's guess. Rod doesn't have to send six even though the spaceship will hold that many. He might decide that he needs everyone else here."

"Are you ladies talking about me behind my back?" Rod joked as he entered the cafeteria and sat down beside the two.

"We were just guessing who else might be going back to Earth on The Seeker," responded Sandy. "Since you are in charge, your name came up."

"I'm still communicating with Earth about that. I wish you'd change your mind and stay, Sandy. We're really going to miss you."

"Not a chance, Rod. I've had my fling. Now it's time to settle down, back on Earth."

An uncomfortable silence descended upon the three, while they imagined life at Terra Nova sans Sandy Maloney. Finally Rod coughed. "Not to change the subject," he began, "but I've been looking for Galveston. Have either of you seen him?"

"Nope," replied Sandy.

"Uh, I saw him early this morning in here," stammered Larraine.

"Well, if you see him again, tell him I'm looking for him."

Sandy and Larraine finished eating and headed back to the greenhouse. As they strolled along, Sandy slyly inquired,

"Why do I get the feeling that you weren't being entirely honest with Rod?"

Larraine feigned innocence. "What do you mean?"

"I think you know more about Rory Galveston that you let on. You don't lie very well, Larraine."

"I didn't lie," insisted Larraine.

"Were you entirely truthful to Rod?"

"I suppose not," admitted Larraine.

"So where is Mr. Geologist?"

"He went out to the cave," whispered Larraine with trepidation.

"By himself?"

"Yes." Larraine was miserable as she made excuses. "What's he supposed to do when Commander Sherman won't ever let him go out there?"

"Larraine, I'm not saying I agree with the stance Rod is taking on this, but Rory should know better than to go out there by himself."

"I can't tell on him," Larraine pleaded.

"It's too late now anyway, but Rod will find out. And when he does, I don't want to be anywhere near Rory Galveston."

"What can Commander Sherman do to him?" wondered Larraine, parroting Rory's question of the morning.

"Larraine, Rod is the commander of the base. He can lock him up, demote him, and send him back to Earth. Those are just for starters. Rory is not being very smart about this."

The two women spent the afternoon working together among the plants. Larraine did her best to concentrate on the vegetation, but thoughts of Rory plagued her mind. At sunset, Sandy suggested they call it a sol. Carefully checking the temperature settings one last time, the two looked out at the gathering shadows. The stark contrast of black against the brilliantly lit ochre cliff walls from the setting Sun thrilled the viewers.

Against the backdrop created by the sunset, the silhouettes of Rory Galveston and N3 stood out. They were almost back to the robot and rover shed, and Larraine breathed a sigh of relief, seeing that Rory was back to Terra Nova safely. She still sympathized with the plight of the geologist, even though she felt guilty for not being completely truthful with Rod.

Uh-oh, groaned Larraine inwardly as she looked toward the cluster of cylindrical habitats. For out of the airlock scrambled Rod Sherman, and even inside his pressurized suit, his figure clearly seethed with anger.

CHAPTER 22

PREPARATIONS

Rory had angered Rod many times before, but even he was surprised by the commander's vehemence. Rod had not even let him display his geological samples, electronic photos, or notes, before lambasting him. "You're out of here, Galveston," Rod raged, as they met in the rover shed.

Pavel and Andrew tried to pretend that they hadn't overheard, but they heard all right. Anyone with a pressurized suit on heard loudly and clearly through their head sets.

He can't mean it, Rory told himself. *With Sammy going home, he has no other geologist here. UNSEF won't let him send me home. They need geological data, and I'm the only one who can give it to them.*

Rory had returned to his pod and rested on his bunk as his imagination ran wild. It was only a matter of time before the others turned in for the night. The pod would be even more uncomfortable than usual with all of them knowing. After tossing and turning in agony for awhile, Rory got up and sulked into the communications center. He wanted to talk with the only person who might understand what he had done.

Tony was clearly uncomfortable as he saw Rory enter his domain. *He's already heard,* thought Rory. Aloud, he said, "I want to contact Hope, Tony."

"Has Rod okayed it?" asked Tony cautiously.

Rory nearly exploded. "No, Davis, he hasn't. Do I really need his permission to talk to my friend, Sammy, up there?"

"Technically, yes," answered Tony, "but if you'll make it quick, I'll connect you."

"Whatever. Don't do me any favors." Rory's sarcasm was evident.

"You know," began Tony, "you could do with an attitude modification. No one on Mars is out to get you."

"Right. Don't give me a lecture. Just let me talk to Sammy."

Tony put the call through. "Terra Nova to Hope. Come in, please."

Scott's voice could be clearly heard. "This is Hope."

"I have Rory Galveston here, and he'd like to talk with Sammy Yoon. Could you get Sammy?"

"Sure. Just a minute."

There was an uncomfortable silence between Rory and Tony as they waited for Sammy's voice. Finally, they were both relieved to hear it. "Sammy here. Who's calling?"

Tony indicated that Rory should pick up the com-link.

"Hey, Sammy," Rory began. "It's me. How's it going?"

"Hey, Galveston. Good to hear from you. Things are great. I've even been doing a little jogging up here. I'm almost 100 percent. It looks like the good doctor was right, and I'm deathly allergic to the Martian dust that we know and love."

"I'm glad you're getting well, Sammy," Rory said in honesty. Sammy was the one person besides himself within millions of kilometers that he actually cared about.

"So what's new down there? Have you been out to the cave?"

"Yes." Rory proceeded to give Sammy the details about his trip, including his discovery of a second cave entrance, but leaving out his run-in with Rod. He knew Sammy would be savoring all the geological information he could get. "I think the silo's walls are obsidian, but I haven't had time to run any tests on the specimens I took."

"That's pretty exciting, Buddy," exulted Sammy. "It could prove that we have a volcano under the ice cap and could even be a source of water."

"I know," agreed Rory. Tony was beginning to make a cutting motion across his throat, indicating that Rory should end the call. "I have to go now, Sammy, but I'll keep you informed."

"Thanks, friend," answered Sammy. "I'm really hungry for any information you can give me about Mars. I wish I could be there to help you out."

"So do I, Sammy. So do I. Catch you later."

At the beginning of the next week, Rod posted the crew roster for The Seeker. To no one's surprise, Brian Delaney would pilot the craft back to Earth, with Dmitri Nazarov as navigator. Sandy Maloney would also be on-board, assisting the crew with any of its medical problems. Rounding out the crew would be geologists Sammy Yoon and Rory Galveston.

Terra Nova reeled with the news about Rory. They found it hard to believe that Rod would send both geologists packing. However, all agreed that Rory had pushed him to the limit and none, except Larraine, would be sorry to see him go. Rory Galveston only cared about Rory Galveston. He was reckless, endangering himself and others with his careless, thoughtless actions, and Terra Novans believed they would be better off without him.

So five people would be returning to Earth. In two years, another crew of six would be arriving to add to Terra Nova's population. The settlement could very well do without a geologist for that long.

Larraine wished there was something she could say to console Rory, but he refused to talk with anyone. He kept to himself, ignoring any efforts by others to communicate with him. Larraine wasn't sure how she felt about the situation. She agreed that Rory was in the wrong, but he had a good reason. She couldn't deny her attraction to the handsome young scientist. *A totally hopeless crush,* she thought. *I'm way too young, and he is far too good looking to care about me.*

Rory clearly felt sorry for himself and was unrepentant about his actions. He blamed Rod Sherman for picking on him. *If it was anyone else, Rod would have made sure they got to investigate the cave. He just had it in for me.* Rory determined that if he could not continue to explore, no one else would benefit from his samples. He packed them to take back to Earth, where he would subject them to much better tests than were possible on Mars.

Sandy anticipated the return to Earth with excitement. Fourteen months long, every minute the trek would bring her closer to home and her husband. She missed him so much. She had little to take with her besides her memories of living in an exotic, wild, primitive, wonderful world and electronic pictures that everyone on Earth had already seen. She felt good, knowing that largely because of her efforts, food would be plentiful on Mars for the foreseeable future. She had accomplished fine work on this planet, and she felt proud of herself. *I couldn't be leaving it in better hands,* she thought. *Hiro Tatsuda and Larraine Temple will be a great team.*

Dmitri Nazarov was more than ready to go. By the time The Seeker touched down on Earth, it would be four full years since he had left. His youngest child had only been three years old. *Will she remember me? Will they be glad to have me back?* Dmitri knew he would be glad to be home. In fact, he wondered why he had ever wanted to go to Mars. *Four years of my life gone, and for what? Have I really made a difference here?*

Sammy Yoon sorted through mixed feelings. His work on Mars was unfinished, and he longed to spend more time with his explorations and investigations. However, he could not refute the fact that being off of the surface of Mars had dramatically improved his health. He was nearly back to normal. Obviously, he could not survive on Mars. *Maybe I can work with samples sent to Earth from Mars,* Sammy promised himself.

Brian Delaney was not sorry to be heading home. In his forties, Brian had curly blond hair, and attractive blue eyes. He was still single, but searching for the right person. Clearly, he wasn't likely to meet her on Mars. *I've had the adventure of a lifetime,* he surmised. *Now it's time to get back to reality.*

Healthy again, Dieffenbachia Bateman savored the idea of the trip to Hope. She would be climbing on the shuttle with the others, to take Scott's place on the Orbiter. They would have a short two sols on Hope, and then Scott would pilot the shuttle back to Terra Nova. *Is there any chance to rekindle the feelings we once had for each other?* Diff had never stopped caring about Scott, even when he hurt her so badly. *Is there still a chance for us, Lord?* Once again, Diff surprised herself. Conversing with God seemed natural and necessary to her now.

At the end of the week, Larraine joined most of the settlement's inhabitants to watch the shuttle leave. Blasting down the graveled runway, it rocketed skyward leaving Terra Nova literally in the dust. Tears rolled down her cheeks as she fought to bring her emotions under control. She would miss Sandy Maloney who had become so much more than a tutor. Having spent hours studying with the botanist, she had come to appreciate Sandy's spirituality and truly considered her a friend. *Can I really help take care of the greenhouse without Sandy's leadership?* She also agonized over Rory's leaving. While she had to admit that he seemed to only care about himself and his work, she knew that underneath his tough exterior, there was more to the young scientist. She had seen glimpses of his humanity in his concern for Sammy. She also sensed that he was not convinced of his agnosticism. She had just barely begun to know Rory, and now he was leaving. She would probably never see him again. *I wish I could have been able to get to know him better.* Even though Larraine knew that Rory was too old for her, he was the closest person in Terra Nova to her age besides Andrew. There was no denying her attraction for him.

Larraine turned to head back to the greenhouse, saying a prayer for those returning to Earth. *Lord, please protect them and take them safely to Earth. Give them patience with each other on their long journey, and if it be your will, let us all meet again some day.*

Trailing Hope in orbit for a short while, the shuttle caught and docked with the larger craft. Brian shut down the engines and turned to his four passengers. "Well, we've just completed the first step in our journey home." All cheered except Rory, who ignored the others and stared out the viewing port at the planet below them until the airlock outer doors enclosed the shuttle.

Dmitri opened the shuttle door into the Orbiter's airlock, and one by one, the passengers clambered inside. The shuttle door closed with a *whoosh* and the airlock pressurized. Finally, Scott opened the Orbiter door from inside, as Sammy and Chang stood by to greet the Earthbound visitors and Dieffenbachia Bateman. The three were enthused to have visitors.

Scott was especially eager to see Diff and renew their friendship. *Has she truly forgiven me? Will she be glad to see me?* Even though the five passengers were all still dressed in their pressurized suits, Diff was easy to pick out. She was so tiny compared to anyone else that there was no mistaking her. As she removed her helmet and pulled her curly red hair out of its ponytail, Scott thought her breathtaking.

Diff's vivid green eyes held Scott's ebony black ones, as time stood still for the two former friends. Each called up cherished memories while they smiled at each other. Neither noticed that everyone else had already cleared the airlock and were being shown to their quarters by Sammy and Chang.

"It's good to see you, Diff," gulped Scott.

Diff's smile lit up her face as she responded, "I'm glad to see you too, Scott. Have you taken good care of my Orbiter?"

"Your Orbiter?" Scott pretended astonishment. "I thought Hope belonged to UNSEF."

"Well, UNSEF thinks so, but she's really mine," joked Diff.

Scott became serious. "Diff, have you really forgiven me?"

"I really have, Scott," Diff assured him. "I want us to be friends again."

"I want us to be more than friends."

"That might happen," mused Diff, "but for now, let's work on our friendship."

"I can live with that," Scott agreed, his dark face brightening with the hope in his heart.

"Ahem. Captains Jamison and Bateman, could you give the crew a little of your attention?" interrupted a jovial Chang Lee, who had returned to the airlock, looking for them.

"It's nice to see you too, Chang," teased Diff. "We thought *you* were taking care of the crew."

Scott and Diff finally left the airlock and walked into the Orbiter. "I've been staying in the captain's quarters," said Scott, "but I'll move out so you can have them tonight."

"That's not necessary, Scott," replied Diff. "I'll stay with Sandy until you return to Terra Nova. I'd like to spend some time with her before she leaves for Earth."

"UNSEF wants them to leave in about 48 hours. We don't know the exact hour yet, but we'll be informed of it in the next 24," Scott explained. "As you've already been informed, right after they leave, Rod wants me to shuttle down to Terra Nova. You and Chang will be staying here."

As Diff, Scott, and Chang went to the control deck, the other passengers were making themselves comfortable.

Rory and Sammy were glad to see each other. Amazed at how healthy Sammy looked, Rory marveled, "Hey man, you look great."

"I feel great too," Sammy said. "It looks like Dr. Temple's diagnosis was right. I sure hate to leave Mars, though."

"You and me both," agreed Rory.

"What happened?"

"You know that Rod never liked me," complained Rory. "I went out to the cave alone again, and he blew up. He's using it as an excuse to get rid of me."

"Going by yourself is a pretty serious infraction, Rory. You shouldn't have done it."

"If I'd known this would happen, I wouldn't have gone. It's like he set me up, Sammy. Rod wouldn't let me take anyone with me, and I had nothing to do. The mystery of the cave just kept calling me out there. I tried to resist, but I finally gave in."

Sammy sympathized, "I probably would have done the same thing. It sure wasn't right for him to keep you grounded like that." He brightened, "But I can't say I'm sorry to have your company for the next 14 months."

Rory's shoulders sagged. "I don't know what I'm going to do, Sammy. I doubt if UNSEF or even NASA will let me work for them any more. I really don't want to go home."

"I wish you could stay too," Sammy agreed. "Since you're here, fill me in on all the details of the cave. You only whetted my appetite during that short call the other night."

"What do you want to know?" asked Rory, as he settled in to tell his story.

Meanwhile, Diff had joined Sandy in the lounge. "I'm going to miss you, girl," Diff told her honestly.

"Likewise, Diff," replied Sandy, "but you're in good hands now that you've made friends with Jesus. He's the best friend you could ever have, and he'll always be with you. And now you have Scott too."

"What do you mean?"

"It's pretty obvious that you and Scott are an item."

"Well, we are friends," admitted Diff.

"Whatever you say," Sandy's eyes glinted knowingly.

At the same time, Scott and Brian examined The Seeker. "I've spent some time this month going over her, and she's in good shape," Scott was assuring the other pilot. "We had some hull damage on our way out here, but we were able to repair it, and everything looks good to go. Chang and I fired up the engines, and everything checks out perfectly. She's a good ship, and she'll see you safely home."

"I don't doubt it," agreed Brian, as they entered and looked around. "She sure is a step up from the ship I rode out here. Believe it or not, The Seeker looks quite roomy."

"About three months into your trip, you won't think so."

"You're probably right about that."

Scott took Brian to the craft's storage area and showed him that The Seeker was well stocked with food, water, and air for the journey. Since the craft would leave from orbit, it would not need massive amounts of fuel to escape Martian gravity, and the ship would rely mainly on orbital mechanics to get itself back to Earth. Even so, the fuel tanks had been topped off for maneuvering and making course corrections, as well as docking with Earth's space station.

Brian was impressed. "It looks like you guys have things ship-shape for us. I hope you won't mind if I double check everything tomorrow?"

"I'd think you weren't a very good pilot if you didn't," said Scott.

At that moment, Chang's excited voice interrupted over the Orbiter speaker system. "Scott, Brian, where are you? Get up to the control center right now. There's exciting news from Terra Nova."

Scott and Brian looked at each other. What could this news be? They quickly closed up The Seeker and rushed to the control center. There was barely room to fit in, as everyone else was already there, and they were obviously celebrating something. The control center positively glowed with expectation.

"What's going on?" asked the two pilots.

Diff couldn't stand still. As she jumped up and down, she threw her arms around Scott and exulted, "Terra Nova just heard from Jenny and Pierre. They found water at Red City—an underground reservoir of liquid water!"

CHAPTER 23

WATER!

The mood at Terra Nova was jubilant. Finding water was definitely one of the most important feats ever accomplished on the Red Planet. Even Rod was in a grand mood as he strutted into the communications center to take a call from Red City. He ecstatically greeted Tony Davis and Sally Evanoff, who were already there.

"What a sol!" he exulted. "All of our effort has finally paid off. I had just about decided that the satellite neutron studies indicating subsurface water reservoirs at the North Pole were wrong. How many holes have we dug out there, anyway?"

"Too many," agreed Sally, "but this last hole has definitely met a sizable body of water underground. There is no doubt. Pierre, Jenny, Aaron, and Max are working hard to cap the hole, because as you know, the water immediately becomes gas in the atmosphere as it reaches the surface. We don't want to lose any more of the precious liquid than we have to."

"You do realize that this means there are probably more underground reservoirs on the planet?" Rod was excited. "Neutron studies seemed to show lots of water underground in the southern hemisphere. With this discovery, UNSEF will soon be planning to start other settlements besides Terra Nova."

"I think you're right, Rod," answered Sally, "but just

because we know the water is there doesn't mean it's going to be easy to actually find it. Look how long we've been working at Red City."

"I hate to interrupt," interjected Tony, "but Jenny has been standing by to talk with Rod. Are you ready, Commander?"

In response, Rod grabbed the com-link and began speaking, "This is Rod, Jenny. What's up?"

Jenny laughed. "You must really be feeling good, Rod. Since when do you not use standard protocol on the com-link?"

"I think a little exuberance is in order, Ms. Colfax."

"I can't argue with that," agreed Jenny.

"So I'll ask again, what's up?" Rod winked at Sally.

"What's up is that we need more help out here, Rod. The four of us are working around the clock getting this well capped. We're good engineers, but we could definitely use additional geological know-how out here. Not to mention, we need more people."

"Well, that's a problem," Rod said. "I can't spare any of the personnel here in Terra Nova, and I don't have any geologists to send you."

"The Seeker hasn't left for Earth yet, has it Rod?" Jenny reminded him.

"What are you suggesting?" Rod frowned, not liking the direction the conversation was taking.

"I'm suggesting that you return Rory Galveston to Terra Nova and then send him out here."

"There is no way on Mars that I'm keeping that guy around." Rod was adamant.

Sally grabbed the com-link from Rod and said, "We'll call you back, Jenny. Stand by." Then she handed the com-link to Tony, put her hands on her hips, and faced Rod.

"What?" he asked.

"It is time to swallow your pride, Commander." Rod had never heard Sally speak so forcefully before. "Red City needs help, and you know that Galveston is the answer. Don't deprive them of his help just because you don't like the man."

"It isn't a matter of not liking him. He doesn't follow rules, and he jeopardizes the safety of himself and others. Besides, I tried to send him to Red City in the past, and he refused it."

Sally was not backing down. "Send him out to Red City, and he'll be too worn out to do any solitary exploration. Put Pierre in charge of him. That way he isn't your responsibility. He's not likely to refuse Red City if it means he can stay on Mars."

"I don't like it," argued Rod. "It will undermine my authority. If he won't cooperate, we're stuck with him for at least two years. Plus, I will probably be retiring and heading back to Earth on the next trip, and if Galveston goes then, I'll be stuck in a spacecraft with the jerk for fourteen months."

Sally smiled. "When you retire, I'll be in charge. I promise that I won't let Rory go back to Earth on the same flight as you."

Rod was still unconvinced. "Even so, letting him come back makes it seem like I don't mean what I say."

Sally shook her head. "No it doesn't, Rod. Red City is begging you to do this. You need to do what's best for the people living on Mars and not punish all of us because you're stubborn."

"I can't call him back, Sally," insisted Rod. "I just can't do it."

"Then let me do it. I'll make sure he knows it isn't your idea. I'll lay down the law. Pierre is in charge of him. He'll be staying at Red City, and we expect him to comply with regulations."

Rod gave up. With a great sigh, he finally agreed. "Okay, make the call, Sally. However, I refuse to take the responsibility for Rory Galveston. It will be your job to keep him in line. I'm writing all of this up in the Commander's Log."

"Agreed," said Sally with relief. As Rod Sherman grumpily left the communication center, she turned to Tony and smiled. "Get me Jenny again."

"Gladly," Tony grinned. "Red City, this is Terra Nova. Sally Evanoff is calling Jenny Colfax."

"I'm here," Jenny's anxious voice responded.

"Good news, Jenny," Sally's optimistic outlook was returning. "We're going to get Rory Galveston for you."

"I don't know how you talked Rod into it, but thank you Sally." The relief in Jenny's voice was evident.

"I hope you still feel grateful after you've put up with him for awhile. You might be sorry we did this," warned Sally. "I'm going to contact Hope now, so we can get this in the works. It sure is a good thing you guys didn't find the water a couple of sols from now."

"Let me know when we can expect him," said Jenny.

"I'll keep you informed. I'm signing off now. Terra Nova over and out."

Tony shook his head in amazement. "I don't know how you pulled that one off, Commander Evanoff. I was right here listening, and I still can't believe it."

"Rod's not as tough as he acts," Sally stood up for the commander. "Besides that, he knows it's the right thing to do. Don't judge him too harshly, because being in charge of this settlement is an awesome responsibility that he takes very seriously. In the ten years that he's been in charge, not one life has been lost at Terra Nova. That's partly due to his rules and regs."

"I can't argue with that," replied Tony, "but I can see why some people have a hard time getting along with him."

"I just hope I can do half the job he's done when I'm in charge. Now let's get Hope on the com-link before The Seeker leaves."

"Right," agreed Tony. He opened the com-link and directed the call to the Orbiter. "Terra Nova calling Hope. Come in, please."

Chang's cheerful voice came through loud and clear. "Hey, Terra Nova. What can we do for you this good sol?"

Tony grinned. Chang Lee always made a person feel good. "Commander Evanoff needs to talk with Rory Galveston. Could you please get the good geologist for her?"

"The last time I looked, he was between a rock and a hard place," Chang quipped as Tony and Sally groaned. "I'll see if I can pry him out."

A few minutes passed, but eventually they heard Rory's voice. "This is Rory Galveston. What do you want?" The geologist's voice was as cold and hard as steel.

Sally took a deep breath and began forcefully. "Dr. Galveston, you have a chance to redeem yourself if you are willing."

"What do you mean?"

"I mean that our personnel at Red City have requested your help, and Commander Sherman and I are willing to provide them with it *if* you agree to certain stipulations."

"I don't want to help at Red City."

"Dr. Galveston, you need to change your attitude." Sally's pretty blue eyes were serious. "We all know that you don't really want to go back to Earth. You are being given a chance to stay and continue your work on Mars."

Rory was obstinate. "Helping at Red City is not why I was sent to Mars. It is not included in my job description."

"It's the job that we have available for a geologist right now." Sally proved she could be as immovable as a Martian boulder. "You can take it, or leave it and head for Earth."

Sensing her firmness, Rory began to soften. "How long will I have to stay out there?"

"As long as it takes," Sally was clearly in charge. "You will do everything that Pierre LaSalle tells you to. You will be under his control."

"I don't much like this," complained Rory.

"I don't care whether you like it or not," answered Sally.

"You can have an important piece of helping establish a usable Martian water source, or you can go back to Earth, having accomplished nothing. It's up to you."

Rory was being offered an incredible opportunity, and he knew what his answer would be, but pride kept him from giving in easily. "I'll need some time to think about it," he demanded.

"You don't have much time, Dr. Galveston. The Seeker leaves in 12 hours, and Scott will be returning to Terra Nova on the shuttle right after it goes. Will you be on The Seeker or the shuttle?"

"I don't know," Rory lied.

Sally smiled as she told him, "Well, I hope you make up your mind before Commander Sherman changes his. This is Terra Nova signing off."

As she put down the com-link, she heard Rory's desperate voice saying, "Wait!"

"Turn it off," she directed Tony, and he gladly complied. "Let him stew awhile. We'll call him back in about six hours."

At the end of the sol, Andrew was escorted back from the rover shed by Pavel, and he couldn't wait to share the news with his sister. He left his pressurized suit in the closet near the airlock and scurried back to the Temple dwelling, knowing that the other three members of his family were waiting for him so they could have dinner together. He burst through the door, positively glowing in his canary yellow jumpsuit, alive with the anticipation of sharing the good news with Larraine.

"Rainy! Where are you?"

"Where could I possibly be in this overgrown can?" growled his sister sarcastically. "I'm right here, just like everyone else. It's pretty hard to hide in one tiny room."

Damaris and Preston Temple knew that something was bothering their daughter. Moodiness and sarcasm were just not like her. They knew that she missed her friends and her former lifestyle, but she had been thriving with her new responsibilities.

They were disappointed with her dismal attitude of the past few sols.

Andrew was excited, and even Larraine's disdain could not dampen his spirit. "I have really terrific news. It will stop your moping around."

"I'm not moping around," Larraine argued.

"Whatever," Andrew shrugged. Then brightening up, he gleefully asked, "Guess who's not going to Earth?"

"You and me, that's for sure," grumped Larraine.

"Larraine, what is the matter with you?" asked Damaris.

"I'm just not in a good mood," complained Larraine, "and I don't feel like playing guessing games."

"Well, you'll feel better when I tell you this, Rainy." Andrew's smile lit his green eyes dramatically. "Rory Galveston is coming back to Terra Nova on the shuttle with Scott."

The news hit Larraine like a Martian dust storm, spinning her thoughts crazily. *Could it be true? How can this be possible. No. Andrew is mistaken. There is no way Commander Sherman would let him come back.*

Preston Temple took the words out of Larraine's mouth before she could verbalize them. "Are you sure, Andrew? How can that be possible?"

"Everybody in Terra Nova is talking about it. The engineers at Red City asked for him, and Sally Evanoff talked Rod into it. So he's coming back to help at Red City."

"That's Commander Sherman to you, young man," Damaris reprimanded her son. "You should not call him by his first name."

Larraine was still not quite sure she believed Andrew. "I don't think even Commander Evanoff could convince Commander Sherman to let Dr. Galveston stay."

"It's true, I tell you," insisted Andrew. "Let's go to dinner, and you'll find out. Just ask anyone."

The Temples expectantly traipsed out to the dining area,

but even before they got there, it was obvious that something newsworthy had happened. The very hallways seemed to resonate with exhilaration. As they entered the cafeteria, the people already there were abuzz with the news. "Have you heard?" echoed from person to person.

"Then it's true?" Preston asked Pavel Stanislof.

"Yes. Can you believe it? Rod Sherman is going to let Rory Galveston stay on Mars." Pavel showed as much surprise as everyone else. Everyone knew Rod to be strict in enforcing the rules of the settlement, and they had never known him to forgive anyone for breaking those rules. In fact, Rory was the first person to ever try breaking a rule twice. Because of his stubbornness, Terra Novans questioned his supposed genius level IQ.

Damaris was thoughtful. "Well, I'm glad that Rod is strict. The rules protect all of us, but I'm also glad that he was willing to put the good of the settlement above his judgment of Rory Galveston. I think this will be a good thing for all of us."

"I agree," stated Pavel. "That is, if Pierre can control the young rebel."

"Well, he'll be too far from the cave to take off by himself," pointed out Preston.

"That's true," agreed Pavel. "Let's just hope he doesn't make any other geological discoveries out there, so he will concentrate his energies on helping the citizens of Red City."

Larraine was too lost in her thoughts to eat much of the sweet potato casserole prepared by Sachiko Tatsuda. *Rory Galveston is staying! Even if he is all the way out at Red City, that's better than Earth. Plus, he has to come in now and then. Surely Commander Sherman will have to give him breaks just like everyone else.* She smiled to herself. Things had definitely improved. Not that she believed Rory Galveston had any interest in her, but who knew in a couple of years? Besides, the geologist was interesting to talk to. And maybe she could persuade Commander Sherman to allow another field trip to the cave. Why not, if he had already given in on letting Rory Galveston stay? Yes, the outlook at Terra Nova had definitely changed for the better.

CHAPTER 24

NEW HOPES

The discovery of a natural source of liquid water was definitely the biggest thing to ever happen on Mars since the touchdown of the first explorers some twenty years before. Once controlled and piped, manufacturing water would no longer be necessary, and the abundant source also meant a more easily producible and plentiful supply of oxygen. The crew at Red City was exhausted but elated. They had successfully capped the water supply. The challenge now facing them was to run a pipeline of water the 40 kilometers from Red City to Terra Nova. It was not an impossible task, but it would take time. Producing their own pipe from the raw materials available on the planet provided a clear challenge that they welcomed.

The Seeker left on schedule with four people aboard, beginning its fourteen month journey back to Earth. While the travelers were missed by all, their safety so far reassured the Terra Novans.

Scott Jamison returned to Terra Nova, piloting the shuttle, with an unrepentant but subdued Rory Galveston on-board. It seemed they barely touched down when Pavel Stansilof loaded up Behemoth and transported the two out to Red City. Pavel returned the next sol with Jenny Colfax and Aaron Abrahamson to allow them a few sols respite. Although Pierre was due for a break, he had no desire to leave their glorious find, and he also felt it was his duty to oversee Rory for awhile, as promised.

Pierre was delighted to see Scott again, and excitedly informed him that they found the water supply at the very hole where they had been drilling when the dust storm arose. So Scott had actually been there at the beginning, even though they weren't able to lower a vacuum capsule at the time.

Pierre and Max welcomed Rory, but he remained aloof and sullen at first. All hoped that he would realize the important contribution he was capable of making to the team and overcome his selfish and childish attitude. The crew appreciated his knowledge of geology, and expected him to share his understanding for the work ahead of them.

Scott, pleased to be at Red City once again, looked forward to helping establish the water supply. He had long ago forgiven Pierre for deserting him and Diff and had no doubt that Pierre would come through the next time they faced an emergency. The Frenchman had been completely ashamed and saddened by his behavior, and his help with Diff afterward had gained Scott's respect. Thoughts of Diff filled Scott's mind, and he wondered how he would be able to exist being totally separated from her. He knew he would have to rely on God to help him through. At least they were both sort of on the same planet, and they could see each other occasionally. Scott counted the sols until the next time he had to replace Diff on the Orbiter.

Dieffenbachia Bateman loved being aboard Hope. She welcomed the solitude, especially now that she wanted time to study the Bible. At times when loneliness kicked in, she could always depend on Chang to uplift her spirits. She enjoyed orbiting, and she knew that she and Chang would be replaced by Scott and Tony in a few weeks. Scott. She definitely missed Scott. She wondered where their friendship might lead. It was probably good that they were separated right now, because Diff felt the need to reestablish her feelings for Scott slowly and carefully.

The feelings were definitely there, but could she really trust him yet?

Hardly noticing that Rory was back on Mars, Rod Sherman continued to be stressed and weighted down with the concerns of the growing outpost. He relied more and more on Sally Evanoff's help, recognizing that he could not continue to handle all of the responsibilities alone. Sally was pleased that Rod was giving her more duties, believing that she would be a better leader when the time came.

On the next Sunday, several of the citizens of Terra Nova gathered in the upstairs loft to worship. It had been a bountiful year, and those present recognized the hand of God directing their small settlement.

During the worshipful atmosphere, Damaris and Preston Temple expressed gratitude for the safety provided to their family. They had been protected from a meteoroid swarm, a drastic cave accident, a Martian dust storm, and other dangers that occurred naturally at an alien station, millions of kilometers from Earth. They praised God for continuing to bless and care for their family. It was hard to believe that nearly nine months had passed since they left Earth.

The Terra Novans concluded their worship service by singing one of Larraine's favorite songs, "Blest be the Tie that Binds."

Blest be the tie that binds
Our hearts in Christian love.
The fellowship of kindred minds
Is like to that above.[1]

She felt thankful for the tightly-knit community, of which she was a part. The people here really cared about each other and watched out for one another. She decided to share her news with her friends back on Earth. Andrew went out to the robot and rover shed with Pavel, and her parents were busy performing their duties, so she enjoyed a quiet time alone in the Temple habitat. Reveling in her privacy, she turned on her computer, attached its foldable keyboard, and began composing a letter to Earth.

Olympus 20, 2045

Dear Marta and Lucy,

This time my letter goes to Marta. Please share it with Lucy. We've been on Mars for more than 6 weeks now, which means I've been gone for close to a year. Actually, nine months to be more exact. The two of you have graduated from High School and gone to the prom, which by the way, I want to hear all about. It's been a long time since I've heard from you. Please write back soon.

I've worked hard in all of my classes, and technically they say I've graduated from high school. Obviously, I haven't completed all of the things I told you I was studying, but Commander Sherman says I am studying at a college level, so I'm finished with high school. I am quite proud of the fact that I learned so much about plants from Sandy Maloney and that I am now trusted in the greenhouse. I work under our horticulturist, Hiro Tatsuda, and I continue to learn a lot from him. There are things like watering and thinning that I do on my own now. Can you believe that? Back on Earth, I hardly noticed plants, and now I am one of the experts here. I'm not sure I was really ready for all this, but I'll sure do my best.

We've already lived through some pretty scary times up here. Andrew fell down a deep pit, but we got him out and he is okay. We had a sudden, wild Martian dust storm, but we knew it was coming ahead of time and were able to stay inside and safe. Afterward, it took a lot of work to clean the dust off all of the solar cells. What a mess! Don't ever complain when you have to dust the furniture. You have no idea!

Remember me telling you about Dieffenbachia Bateman? Well, I was right about her and Scott knowing each other before. I won't go into all the details, but Diff wouldn't have anything to do with Scott, because of something that happened back on Earth. Diff almost died during the dust storm, and Scott rescued her. I don't think even that would have changed Diff's mind about him, but believe it or not, both of them turned their lives over to God. He is fixing up their relationship. I can't wait to see what comes of it.

Andrew and I had a geology field trip to a Martian cave with Rory Galveston. Unfortunately, that's when Andrew had his accident. Now Dr. Galveston is out at Red City working with the remote crew there to control and pipe the water that was found.

I'm sure you've already heard about the discovery of water. Every newspaper on Earth must have jumped on the news and screamed it in their headlines. Can you believe it? It is so incredible. I really didn't think they would ever find water up here. But they did, and that insures the survival of Terra Nova and probably future settlements across the planet.

I'm happy and well, but I can't say that I'm always glad to be here. Sometimes I feel like I'd give anything to be able to walk outside without all the gear on. I'd love to pick some flowers and wade in a bubbling brook. More variety in what I can have to eat would be a treat. Yet in spite of all of those feelings, I must admit that there's an excitement about living in a real frontier even when it's hard. I believe in what we're doing here, and I know that we are helping to make future Mars developments, asteroid mining, and even travel beyond a possibility. That's a pretty awesome thought.

I have at least a year and a half more up here. Then I'll be 19, and Mom and Dad say I can decide for myself whether to stay or go, regardless of what they do. I wonder what I'll choose? I plan to pray about it. In the meantime, I have a job that's as important as any other in Terra Nova, and that's pretty neat. You know that I always did like a challenge. Well, I've got one.

We can't often see Earth from the surface of Mars,

because of the hazy atmosphere, but you can see Mars at least
part of the year. Next time it's visible, take a look, and when
you do, remember that there are people up here, including your
friend. Say a prayer for us.

Write back soon.
Love, Larraine

Larraine took her computer to the communications center so she could send her letter. Tony helped her with the transmittal, and as she shuffled back to the Temple pod, she resolved to continue writing. She had mentally been writing a poem about Mars, and she decided that now was the time to make her thoughts more permanent. In the solitude of the Temple home, she switched the computer on once again and began to compose.

Mars
By Larraine Temple

Mars, the planet most like Earth
To thoughts of alien life gives birth.
Tilted on its axis, it has seasons,
And that's just one of the many reasons
People think life may have been here,
Or even still is, hidden somewhere.
Mars has ice caps of frozen water,
Why not liquid, if it was hotter?
The atmospheric pressure doesn't cater
To water's liquid state of matter.
Water at the surface is solid or gas,
Through the state of liquid it does not pass.
Amazingly though, it exists under,
The surface of Mars, what a wonder!
The planet has awesome physical features.
The Valles Marineris stretches 3000 kilometers.

The Olympus Mons, a gargantuan volcano,
As large as the state of Arizona.
Ancient sites of stream-like erosion,
Impact basins, an empty former ocean?
Its surface is littered with rusted fines
Which become airborne during windy times.
Did life ever exist here? We don't know.
We continually investigate though.
Of this I am quite positive,
If ever a life form here did live
God created it by His Word,
And its being will magnify the Lord.

Larraine stopped and thought. She knew she had a lot more to say, but the poem expressed a start. *I'll continue to add to it,* she smiled as she shut her computer down. Deciding to check on the greenhouse, her countenance lit and her step lightened with joy. The possible existence of Martian life still remained an enigma, but there was no doubt that life was presently flourishing on the Red Planet.

The End

Or is it just the beginning?

(Footnotes)
[1] Public domain

Contact Thelma Ritchie
or order more copies of this book at

TATE PUBLISHING, LLC

127 East Trade Center Terrace
Mustang, Oklahoma 73064

(888) 361 - 9473

Tate Publishing, LLC

www.tatepublishing.com